Brad Manue

MW01042615

Finding Daniel

Finding Daniel

Thank you to my wonderful wife,

and to all of the friends and family who helped me during the last year.

The police filed in and out of our house, most of them wore dark blue uniforms, just like the ones in the movies, dozens of young, white men in dark-blue shirts, epaulets on their shoulders, gray pants with a blue stripe down the side, shiny silver badges on their pockets, each walking through the bedroom to look at me. So many I could not count. A few of them nodded in a silent greeting, a look of concern. Most ignored me, looked into my master bathroom, and left as quickly as they came.

Honestly, I can't remember any of their faces. At one point I almost chuckled. I imagined those wooden dolls that artists use to pose in different positions, an oval head of wood with no face. That's what I saw after the first few patrolmen. Oval wooden faces, smooth with a natural grain pattern where their eyes, nose, and mouth should have been.

I didn't chuckle; I suppressed any emotions other than sadness, desperation, and fear. My wife's child was missing, stolen from our house. Gone like a stray dog that wandered away under the fence through a hole it dug. No trace of where he went or how he disappeared.

A thick man wearing a white, short-sleeved, button-down shirt was asking me questions. I responded appropriately, taking care to repeat the same answers I gave to the other half-dozen people who asked me the exact same questions over the last two hours.

I looked at his puffy face, pockmarked from teenage acne. He had a goatee, and whenever I see a goatee I always think of the same joke: "Hey, nice prison pussy." I didn't say it to him though. I didn't snicker or smile or let the corners of my eyes wrinkle with humor. I sat stoically, forlorn with loss, answering truthfully and in carbon-copy fashion to my previous interviews.

"No, I didn't hear anything."

"I don't know anyone who would have done this."

"I don't have any enemies."

"I'm an orthodontist, we don't have enemies, at least not enemies that steal children."

"Yes, that is the most recent picture."

"I can't be sure, but we looked through the pajamas still here, and we believe they were a white top with a giraffe picture and yellow shorts."

I examined the inquisitor's shirt. It had thin, tan lines that ran vertically. The fabric was not 100 percent cotton. It had a sheen. There were dull yellow stains creeping out from his armpits, despite the muscle undershirt I could see and assumed he wore everyday beneath the thin fabric. He looked like almost every depiction of a middle-aged detective in movies or television. I ran through the chicken or egg argument in my head. Did he see the outfit in a movie and gravitate toward the short-sleeved shirt, or had television shows done their research? Was art imitating life, or had life imitated art?

His breath smelled like coffee. Another person might say it reeked, but reeked is such a dramatic word, and it implies I do not like the smell. I love coffee, was drinking a mug myself, slowly, as if disinterested in anything other than the missing child. I wanted another cup, but was afraid to ask and watch them write in their little books, "cared about coffee more than the kid."

I wondered if my breath was as strong with coffee smell as his was coming back at me.

"We put him down at 7:30, enjoyed a glass of wine, and went up ourselves at 10."

"Well, no, she did not have wine. My wife is an alcoholic. I had a glass of wine, she enjoyed water."

"No, Daniel didn't get up, or at least I did not hear him get up."

"We moved him to a bed a month ago. He could get out of his crib."

"Yes, he can open his door, but cannot work the gate at the top of the stairs."

Another wooden-faced man came through the room. He had a mustache, and I thought that would have made me see his other features, but I still just saw a black mustache on smooth-grained wood.

"You need some more coffee?" Detective Caricature asked. I alternated between calling the burly, short-sleeved-shirt-wearing man a caricature and a stereotype.

It was his first original question in more than ten minutes.

"What?" I feigned confusion, like coffee was the last thing on my mind. I acted as if I didn't realize I was drinking coffee, and I certainly didn't know I was out. "Yeah." I looked at my empty mug. "Yeah, I guess. Whatever."

"Jules, go get the guy some more coffee."

The wooden face with a mustache stepped lively out of my bathroom and grabbed my empty cup.

"Black?"

"What?" Yes, I want it black, but I have to act like I'm not thinking about coffee. "Yeah, black, thanks."

I watched the blue uniform leave the room. I counted the seconds in my head, something to do while I answered questions. I was waiting for the grand finale of questions, the two or three this detective really wanted to ask. He didn't care what time I went to bed, or what I drank, or if my alarm system was on. I waited for my coffee, and I waited for the real questions.

The detective leaned against our dresser, a waist-level piece of furniture about six feet long. I sat on my bed, still in my pajamas. Well, not really pajamas, a white T-shirt and flannel pants, but my version of pajamas.

The bed was unmade underneath me. I purposely did not make it so the police could see that my wife and I shared a bed at night. Both sides of the king were rumpled, obviously used just a few hours ago. The corners flung off and meeting in the middle, like we were folding a paper airplane. Two right triangle patterns of the flat sheet met in the middle of our bed to form a large isosceles triangle.

Jules strolled in with my mug of coffee. I saw the steam rising, which meant someone made another pot. My wife and I were the only coffee drinkers in the house, and I brewed eight cups every morning, four for her, and four for me. I actually made it the night before, using the timer on the coffeemaker. It was part of my routine each night. The pot came on at 6:30 a.m., and turned off at 8:30 a.m. It was 10 a.m., the coffee should have been stone cold, and it should have tasted like crap. My mug was steaming and smelled fresh and delicious.

The cops were drinking my coffee. I don't know why I cared. I shouldn't have cared. I should have made it for them myself when they arrived, asked who wanted some—that would have been the normal thing to do.

I didn't want them in my house, and I certainly didn't want them drinking my coffee.

"I'm sorry?" I was focused on maintaining my sad demeanor, making sure the anger from the police invasion and coffee making did not show, and I missed a question in the process.

He repeated it.

"My wife and I have been married for fifteen years."

"We have twins. They are away at summer camp in New Hampshire. They are twelve."

Here it comes. I could see him take a big windup. He would not have been a good major league pitcher. I knew what was coming. Maybe that was his style. Maybe he didn't care that I saw the fastball grip as opposed to the changeups he had been throwing to this point. Unlike his other questions, he gave a tell, a breath out, an anticipatory act that let me know this was it. I could see why this man was not higher than a detective. I am surprised he made it out of uniform. He should have gotten me the coffee while Jules asked me questions.

I was prepared for the question regardless of the delivery, regardless of being surprised or prepared.

"No, Daniel is not my son. My wife had an affair."

His follow-up question elicited the same response I had given twenty times that morning.

"We're working through it."

I loved Daniel. He was an eighteen-month-old baby boy living in my house, born of my wife, whom I also loved dearly. But, and whenever I said this in my head it sounded as horrible as it felt, I did not love Daniel as if he is my own. I've always heard parents saying that, parents who have adopted, or married and blended a family, or are godparents, or whatever relationship that brings a child not of their loins into their lives. That they love the baby like it is their own.

I loved the baby, but not like he was my baby. I knew what a father's love is supposed to feel like. I had two children for whom I have a father's love, and I did not feel it for Daniel.

I had trouble changing his diapers. People without children might not understand what I mean. I have two children, two wonderful kids, and I changed their diapers. I never thought twice about it. I didn't care about the smell or the mess. I did not care about getting peed on when the cold air hit their exposed groins. None of that mattered with my twins.

I hated changing Daniel. The smell revolted me. Wiping his behind was excruciating. Every time I picked him up I felt like I was picking up a friend's child, not my own child, and on top of that, the parent wasn't even my friend. It was my wife's friend, who had a baby and handed the boy to me, and now I was expected to change the smelly diaper.

I thought it would get better, that I would grow to love him the way I was supposed to love him. That I would eventually forgive him like I forgave my wife, but it had not happened yet. I still got mad when he threw food at the wall, or yelled while I was watching television, or did any of the normal stuff an eighteen-month-old does.

I acted like he was some kid visiting my house on a play date. It drove my wife crazy, the way I acted toward Daniel. It was the last thing we were "working through."

"You talk to him like he's the neighbor's kid," Janelle, my wife, would tell me. She had sadness in her voice, disappointment, like I was supposed to know how to deal with the situation. Like I was supposed to look at this child and love him unconditionally without thought of how he came into the world. Like I was supposed to forget that he was a constant reminder of her lost year, her alcoholism, her gambling, her infidelity.

"Is he?" That's what I said the first six months. It was mean, and petty, and evil, but that's how I felt. I still said it in my head, and though I didn't say it out loud, Janelle knows me well enough to hear it rattling between my ears. Like the prison pussy comment. She probably thought the same thing when Detective Stereotype came into the kitchen to question her "separately." If she didn't smile at the joke herself, she smiled at the thought of me saying it to this random policeman in our house, drinking my coffee, and trying to find her child.

"Nice prison pussy."

"Is he?"

I am such an asshole.

The detective asked me other questions, things I expected him to ask, not because they were obvious, but because I had been interrogated for what seemed like hours as I sat in my comfortable clothes on the edge of my unmade bed.

"No, I have not adopted him. We cannot get the father to sign off on the adoption."

"Yes, we've tried."

"Is it awkward?" The question was not new, but the phrasing was. "Awkward is wearing the same shirt and tie as a job interviewer. This was difficult to impossible at first, but we are working through it." I defaulted to my fallback answer; it was also the truth. Janelle and I had not worked through it. It wasn't settled, or fine, or great. Daniel and I were a work in progress, but I was doing the work.

"Do I care? No. He's an innocent baby. I love him like he's mine." I knew what to say. Everyone knows what to say.

"Yes, I understand you find that hard to believe, but it's the truth."

"Well, we looked at adopting twelve years ago, before we had the boys, and we explored all the angles. I had no problem back then, and I have no problem now."

Answering this particular line of questioning was upsetting, and I worked hard to contain my anger. I wasn't so much angry at the police for asking me, over and over again. I was upset with myself, because I was lying to them. I did care that Daniel was black, but not for the reasons they most likely believed. I honestly did not care about his race. I cared that he was different from me, that his skin was a constant in-my-face reminder that he wasn't from me.

And that my wife fucked some other guy.

I hated changing Daniel because his mocha skin was under that snow-white diaper, laughing at me, mocking my decision to take back a cheating, gambling, drinking whore.

I decided I was done answering the same questions. I finished my coffee, set the mug on the nightstand, and began the same monologue I had with the previous interviewers.

"Look, I get that I'm a suspect, and I've answered all of your questions. What I don't understand, you've spoken to my wife. She's been with me since yesterday afternoon, literally, never left my side once. I'm sure she's told you, or your partner, or your cohort, or whoever is talking to her. Unless you think we did this together, I'd appreciate it if you started focusing your attention on someone else and found my goddamn kid."

I'd seen the movies and read the books this detective was emulating. It was time for me to display righteous indignation.

"Where could a baby boy go?" The tables were turned, and the detective squirmed uneasily as I continued my questions.

"Well, sir, we have an Amber Alert out."

"I know all that. What I'm asking is, if someone takes a kid, how do they get away with it? How does someone just show up with a little boy? It's not like he's a baby, he's eighteen months. He can talk. He's going to ask questions if he's out in public."

"Well, that's why we put an alert out, so people can call with suspicious behavior," he stuttered back at me.

"And who would target us in our house other than the father's family? Who would pick us other than that convict's parents or sister? Why are you talking to me like I threw Daniel out with the trash, when the people who want Daniel are somewhere else?" That came out wrong, made it sound like I didn't want Daniel. Lucky for me this detective was not very good, he was on the defensive, and he was not taping our conversation.

"What I mean is." Just in case someone else heard, or Detective Short Sleeves' gears started grinding faster. "Janelle and I have won every ruling to keep Daniel. We were sued four times, and to be honest they didn't have the money to sue us. They are desperate to get him. Go lean against their bureau and drink their coffee." It felt good to complain about them drinking my coffee.

"We have a team at their place now," he replied quickly in an attempt to appease me.

"Is it the FBI? I thought the FBI did missing persons cases." Television watching was carrying me a long way in this situation. "And I am going to see my wife. She is a wreck, and I should be with her, but not before I put on some goddamn pants." I went into my closet and selected clothes for the day. Something easy, that I could wear on television if necessary, that would not be too cold in an FBI office or police precinct. I grabbed a pair of khaki linen pants, a dark-blue golf shirt, a belt, some socks, and began to dress in the closet.

I emerged to find Janelle standing in the bedroom. The door was shut, and we were alone, together for the first time since the police pulled us apart three hours ago.

She was the wreck I anticipated. Her eyes were puffy from crying, and her nose was pink around the edges after what was probably endless nose wiping and blowing. It was hard to see her like this, unkempt, blown apart. She was always put together. Always looking good, dressed appropriately, immaculate in appearance, ready for the situation. I marveled at how she did it, and after years of guesswork, had decided it was her hair. She kept her hair looking good, and it disguised so many faults. She had beautiful, dark brown hair, and it was such a stunning feature that it drew a person's eyes away from anything else. Even pulled back into a ponytail, her shiny, healthy hair made Janelle look spectacular in every situation.

Her hair was the first thing she let go when the drinking really started, the first visible indication she was unraveled. The first thing I missed in a series of indicators I should have picked up on. If I had noticed the gray strands of hair, though they were still pulled into a ponytail, or how her hair was getting much longer than she ever let it get when she was going to a salon, I might have thought to check our credit card balances, and I would have seen them maxed out, and then noticed Janelle was draining our vacation fund of cash to pay the minimum on the cards. She used the rest to gamble and drink. It's not like I'm an absent husband. I asked her about the gray once, and she said she was trying a natural look. I glanced at the length, thought the same excuse applied, and moved along.

The big things are easy to see. I checked the credit cards when the fridge went bare for two days. I examined the bank accounts when I found a dent in her car she could not explain and refused to get fixed. Not only did I find the vacation fund empty, and the credit cards maxed, but minor things like our car insurance and life insurance weren't being paid.

The big stuff is easy to spot, but when the big stuff starts happening, it's way too late. She was too far gone, too deep in the hole to pull out. When the big stuff started happening, Janelle wasn't Janelle anymore.

If I had just taken a second to question her hair a second time, the last four years of my life would have been so different.

It hung down this morning, frizzing out on the sides. On the few mornings I woke after her, I saw her hair like this, before she rushed into the bathroom, before she pulled it up tightly into a ponytail with a hair elastic or tugged a brush through it on her way down the stairs to get coffee.

With her hair a mess, I noticed her other minor faults, her puffy eyes, her pink nose, her desperate look. It reminded me of her lost year, of the months she was too hung over to care about her appearance. I instinctively sniffed the air for the hint of cigarettes and booze, indications she spent the night at a bar, casino, or one of the horrific options for drinking and gambling that I didn't even know existed before my wife became an alcoholic gambling addict.

I walked toward my wife, my suffering partner, and enveloped her in my arms. She wept uncontrollably. Her baby was gone. A piece of her, practically an appendage the last eighteen months, ripped from her in the night.

I knew what Daniel meant to Janelle. She did not love him more than our sons, but her love for him was unique. He was her savior, a spark that pulled her out of the abyss that was her life. She was lost, beyond my help, and beyond the rescue of our children. I had filed for divorce. She was out of the house, living who knows where, doing God knows what with who knows whom. I had not seen her for a few weeks. She made an attempt to watch the boys' baseball games from her car for a while, sunglasses on, parked on the other side of the street, peering through the chain-link fence, but she had stopped coming to those too. She skipped our legal meetings, skipped our couples therapy, skipped out on our life.

Until one day Janelle woke feeling sick. She thought she was dying, finally accomplishing her goal of self-destruction, of ending her pain and self-loathing through booze and reckless living.

Instead, she had morning sickness. She was growing a life.

She showed up at my door two weeks later, eight weeks since the last time I had seen or heard from her. Janelle's hair was styled and cut. Gone were the split ends of the previous six months. There were still gray strands of hair, but they looked healthy and shiny, and she was gorgeous again. I can still picture her, standing in a pink gingham shirt, untucked and hanging over her jeans. I noticed her shirt was untucked because it was never untucked. She was a tucked-in-with-a-belt kind of woman. She was thin and tall, never needing to hide a paunch or muffin top; she always displayed her toned, flat belly.

One thing I give Janelle credit for during that lost time, her one unselfish act: She never used a lawyer, never fought me when I threw her out and forbade her from seeing the boys. That morning she knocked on my door was no different. She came to our home alone, hat in hand, and looked at me, smiled like she used to smile, and said, "I'm back. I'm pregnant. I need you. I haven't had a drink in two weeks. I know I don't deserve you, or the kids, or my life, but I need it, and more importantly, I want it."

I stepped aside and let her back into my world.

As I hugged her now and she wept in my arms, I worried that without her anchor, without Daniel she would drift away like she had just a few years earlier. I knew, as I did the moment we frantically searched our house for Daniel, that I wasn't just looking for a little boy. I wasn't just searching for my wife's eighteen-month-old son. I was fighting to keep my wife in my life. I was fighting to keep my twins' mother in their lives. If Daniel was really gone, Janelle wouldn't be too far behind him.

"We're going to get him back," I whispered into her ear.

She squeezed me tighter.

14

"You don't understand," I explained. "I know what he means to you. I know what will happen if he's gone. It means you're gone, and I won't lose both of you. I can't."

Honesty is one of the first things they try to teach you in counseling. They tell you stupid things wrapped up into nice little phrases. At first I thought we had a really shitty counselor, despite her high hourly price tag.

"Be honest with each other."

"Stop lying."

"Open your hearts, let down your walls." That was my favorite. I giggled the first time she "advised" we do that. "Did you listen to Pink Floyd before we came in today?" was my comment.

As I've admitted, I'm an asshole.

I never completely understood what kind of "honesty" bullshit she was pitching. I stupidly thought I was supposed to tell Janelle her outfit looked bad or that I didn't like her haircut. Maybe she was supposed to tell me I had put on a few pounds or she didn't like my deodorant.

"I don't have the answers," I told the expensive counselor one session, raising my voice out of frustration and lack of sleep after Daniel was born. "My wife spiraled into alcohol and gambling addiction right before my eyes, but I sure as hell know that it wasn't because I didn't tell her she had spinach in her goddamn teeth."

The morning Daniel disappeared, as I hugged my wife, I began to understand the honesty the therapist used dozens of idiotic metaphors trying to convey. Janelle knew how I felt about Daniel. If I told her I wanted to get him back because he was the light of my life, that's the kind of bald-faced lie that wrecks a marriage. The honesty I brought to our embrace was the honesty we spent thousands of dollars and hours learning to achieve. Janelle needed to understand that I was in this search with everything I had, and telling her it was for Daniel was a bad lie that she would see though before I finished saying it. I was in this for me, for us, for our twins, for my life. I was in this because I believed Daniel was the glue that held Janelle to me and held her together. In fact, there was no two ways about it. I knew he was the glue, and even though I might not have enough love for Daniel to move heaven and earth to get him back, I let Janelle know I had enough love for everything else in my life to make sure her little boy was coming home.

She loosened her grip and pulled away.

"We are a team on this?" She had every right to ask me. I'd been "good" with Daniel, but I could not say I had been a committed part of the Daniel team.

I held her by the arms, staring into her tear-soaked brown eyes. "Not only are we going to get our son back." I never called him my son, but this morning, that moment, for the first time, I felt it. I finally realized that Daniel wasn't just Janelle's savior, that beautiful, sweet, innocent little boy was my savior. He gave me back my life, my partner, and my family. I owed him.

"Not only will he be back in this house, but I'm going to get the people that did this to us, and I'm going to make sure it never happens again. Whatever it takes, it will never happen again."

I really hoped Detective Television Show had not left a recording device in our bedroom.

If this was a television show or an action movie, this is the time you would find out I used to be in the military, that I was special forces or maybe a ranger. Maybe I am an expert with knives, guns, and explosives.

Maybe I would reveal that I grew up in a rough part of town, got out because of some fluke, and my childhood buddies were all gangsters or criminals, that I had some connection to the underbelly of society, and I would now tap those connections to find Daniel.

Maybe I was a spy and actually still am a secret agent.

Unfortunately, I really am an orthodontist, and if you knew how hard and long a journey it is from high school to running a successful orthodontic practice, you would realize I missed most of the fun in my late teens through early thirties. Truth be told, I started busting my ass in high school. I wanted to attend a great university, and that takes hard work and time. I didn't have a girlfriend until college.

I held a gun once, when I visited a buddy in Mobile, Alabama, and his idea of a good time was going to a gun range. I shot a pistol, a rifle, and a shotgun. That's it. I don't own a knife of any consequence. I live in a safe, nice suburb of Cincinnati. I pay my taxes and assume my money funds a police force that makes weapon ownership unnecessary.

I grew up in Munster, Indiana. There weren't any options for gangster friends. The five people I keep in touch with are pretty wealthy. We were on the swim team, studied hard, helped each other achieve. Two of them work in banking, one owns a micro-brewery, one has six restaurant franchises, and the last one played professional baseball in Houston for seven years. He doesn't work anymore. The six of us take a golfing trip every other year.

As I stood with my wife, having promised to not only find our child but also exact revenge and prevent a future issue, my wheels began to spin. How in the hell was I going to do either?

"I like your outfit," Janelle told me loudly, ending my brainstorming. "Don't ask me how I know, but you'll need a jacket or sweater. Police stations are cold. I think it's part of their tactic, to make suspects uncomfortable." She broke from me to find clothes for herself. She continued to speak from the walk-in closet, her voice raised without concern for other people hearing. "Of course, a lot of the cops are kind of pudgy. Maybe the cool precinct is because they get hot easily. I hope the Rondos are wearing shorts and T-shirts." The Rondos were Daniel's father's family.

She came back out in just a bra and panties. She was brushing her hair. She had wiped her face clean of the tear streaks. "I'm thinking we have two days." Her voice was low this time, and I immediately realized the earlier comments were a ruse. She wanted the police to hear her sound like a wealthy suburban housewife, not a cunning mother with a plan to find her son.

"Two days for what?"

"We have at most forty-eight hours to get him back. I bet whoever took him is still in Cincinnati for a few days, maybe just one day, but I hope two. All of the Rondos will be under suspicion, but one of them will be cleared in forty-eight hours. That person will get Daniel and flee. We have to find him by then or he's gone. I also want to get him back before the twins come home from camp." Janelle pulled a white, V-neck T-shirt over her head. She sat on the bed and began sliding her jeans up each leg.

"I know I just promised to…" She was ahead of me with her ideas. I stuttered as I listened to Janelle's plan.

Janelle cut me off. "We need to look at your clients, see who pays cash. I bet you have some connections that you don't even realize. I'm sure we have people we can reach out to."

Janelle is smarter than I am. People who know us, people who are our true friends, know that she is the genius of the couple. It's easy to forget how bright she is after she gambled half of our money away, and ended up as a wino on the streets for a few months. It's easy to dismiss her intelligence when she tells you she hasn't worked since being fired from a consulting firm in 2008. But do not underestimate a genius mother with a lost child.

"Make the bed." She was back to speaking loudly. "I can't believe you had people in here when the bed was unmade."

I moved to the other side of the room to help her fix the sheets while she continued to describe her plans.

"They will want to see your client list, to go through it with you. Let's get that to them immediately, and you can find your cash-paying clients in the process. Cash payers will most likely indicate criminal activity."

She was good. I nodded like a dumb lackey.

"We are not going to scuttle the police investigation, and we're not going to lie. Our best scenario is that they find Daniel safe. But we also need to take care of business ourselves. I will exonerate you quickly, as I already have downstairs. You need to find a client you can reach out to, develop a strategy this morning, and start your own operation."

"Operation?" I shook my head. "Honey, I'm a goddamn tooth straightener. What do you think I'm going to do? Walk around the streets of the city working through my contacts?"

"Gabe, you're going to get dirty. How dirty? I do not know. You have two days to find my baby." She dropped her eyes. "You've never asked me how low I got, how deep I sank." She raised her face to meet mine across the chasm of our king bed. "You aren't going to like what you find."

"Prison guards," I blurted out, probably a bit too loudly.

"What?" she replied quietly.

"I put braces on a few of the prison guards. Ohio has a fantastic dental policy. Word got around four years ago. Maybe they can lean on Rondo in a way the FBI can't or won't."

"Perfect, that's a good start." We finished the bed. I went to my dresser to retrieve a medium-weight cashmere and cotton sweater. Janelle pulled a light-blue, cable-knit V-neck over her shoulders. We met next to the door.

"I can't promise you'll still love me when this is over, and I hate to sacrifice that to find him." She put her arms around me, kissing me on the lips, closing her eyes. She finished the kiss, and we faced each other, toe to toe, her arms around my waist and mine around her lower back. "But it's a risk I have to take."

"J, if I've stood by you until now, do you know how bad it will have to get for me to walk away?"

She pulled me into a full hug, her lips just under my ear. "Lean on Rondo," she whispered. "He used to rape me when I passed out on the floor. I never cheated on you willingly."

My jaw clenched with anger.

"I was always so drunk." She squeezed my waist. "I never stopped loving you. I stopped loving myself."

A harsh slap of honesty caught me in the jaw.

She pulled away and opened the bedroom door. Three police officers, young men in uniforms, stood outside in our hallway. The one who brought me coffee, mustached Jules, nodded toward me.

Janelle walked to the kitchen downstairs. I stood in place, like a statue, unsure of my emotions after Janelle's information. Rondo raped her? Why did she lie to me? Why didn't she tell me she was a drunk sex doll for that animal? How far gone was she two years ago?

"Are you okay, sir?" Jules touched my arm, seeing I was in a slight daze. His features came into focus, and he no longer wore a wooden puppet face. I saw that his mustache was an attempt to cover the fact that he was young, very young, probably 22. He had a baby face for which his thin mustache could not compensate. Jules was of average height, and his build was slight, adding to his youthful appearance. His short, high and tight haircut was another obstacle his mustache could not overcome.

"I'm far from fine, Jules, my son is missing." I took a step around him. "But—" I paused to meet his eyes. "Thank you for asking, and I thank you all for being here."

The sooner the police found Daniel, the less chance I had of getting dirty and finding out what my wife did for the six months she was out of our house.

I'm sure you think you know desperation. I certainly thought I knew what it was. I've been late for an appointment, stuck in traffic for an important interview, maybe late for a test, and I've felt that pain in my stomach, the urgency we've all felt. A helplessness that no matter what, we are going to be late, the plane is going to take off without us, the test is going to start and I won't get all of my time.

That's not desperation, not even close, not in the same zip code. What I felt that morning, after speaking with my wife, knowing I had two days to find a child when all I possessed was the skill set of an orthodontist, that was desperation. My leg twitched uncontrollably under the table as the FBI team, new additions to the crowd of people in my house, asked Janelle and me all of the same questions we'd been asked over and over again.

I was desperate because up until a few minutes ago, there was nothing I could do. I was relying on the police to find Daniel. I could give information, do any interviews they wanted me to do, make some phone calls, but really, I was in the backseat of the speeding car. Hell, I was in the wayback, the goddamn third row. The police were in the second row, and the FBI was driving. Now? I had to get to my office, look through my files, find the employment information of my prison guard clients, and see if any of them were overseeing Rondo, the son of a bitch who raped my wife.

"You know," I interjected as the red-haired woman in a dark pantsuit paused to write in her notebook. Her badge was clipped to her suit jacket lapel. "FBI," in large blue block letters, told me what she did. "I told the detective that I don't have any enemies, and that's true."

She looked up at me, stopping midword in her notes. I could see half of my wife's name written where her pen stopped, "Janel." I almost smiled.

"Yes?" she said, neither interested in or leading my response. It must have been her training, to maintain an even keel. I bet her pulse remained between sixty and seventy-five no matter what she was doing.

"I might not have enemies, but I might have some known sex offenders or maybe some bad people in my past or present client list. Well, the kids are my clients, but the parents? Perhaps I am a target and don't even realize. Maybe I have an enemy and I just don't know it yet. Orthodontists have the perception of doing well financially. That's a possible motive, right?"

The redhead wore thick-rimmed black glasses, covering her greenish-brown eyes. I doubted the frames were prescription; I've seen the intelligent look before. She was trying to deflect her attractiveness by accessorizing. It was not working. She leaned backward in her chair and spoke to an older agent seated next to her. They had a brief, secret conversation. Their body language did not disclose their decision or mood.

My leg continued to bounce wildly under the table. I was glad it was not a glass top, or the agents would have been suspicious.

She moved forward. "Is your client list online? Can you access it from here?"

"We use a billing system that will give you my clients for the last fifteen years. I have access to my calendar here, but we keep the billing information on a closed server system." I shook my head. "They keep telling me to switch to a cloud system, but I don't want to spend the money."

Janelle put her hand on my shoulder. "Gabe, it's not your fault. None of this is your fault, just do what you need to do." She faced the FBI duo. "Can one of you take him to his office? Do you need us together?"

Damn, my wife was good. She lied so convincingly. It was why I never suspected her problems, never considered she was unhappy, or ten steps way past unhappy, beyond miserable. We always talked, I was involved, I repeat, I was not a distant husband. "You're happy staying home with the kids, right? You don't miss the life?" The life of a management consultant who traveled four to five days a week, ate steak dinners, and worked long hours, who solved important issues and presented to boards and CEOs.

"I love being home." She had smiled. "I don't miss it a bit." She was drunk each and every time she fed me that same bullshit line.

FBI Redhead turned to her partner. He nodded, keeping his focus on me.

"You know what?" I pretended that I had a revelation. "I bet they can print it out, scan it, and email it to me." I wanted a copy for myself, something on my phone to skim through and find the names I needed. "What information do you want, names and addresses?" I led them a little bit more. "I mean, we have just about everything you could imagine, occupations, insurance, of course, marital status, emergency contacts. Do you want the people who didn't have insurance? Maybe they are desperate for cash, are more likely suspects."

Privacy be damned, my son was missing.

The stoic partner nodded. "Give us everything you have on them, but keep the list to the last two years. See if anyone missed some payments. Maybe had you take the braces off early because of financial issues." He had a full head of dark hair with a lot of salt creeping into his pepper on the sides. "You might have received blame for the issues or created embarrassment without knowing it." His expression remained the same. "Let's work this angle quickly."

I took his cue and walked outside to call my practice manager.

My office is a well-oiled machine. If I have to be perfectly honest, I am the number one impediment to it working smoothly. Seven years ago I hired Danette Sweets to run my business operations. She was an associate of Janelle's, working insane hours, traveling Sunday to Friday, and she wanted out. She wanted to start a family. I begged Janelle to run my office for years, pleaded with her every six months as I fired one manager after another. Danette was the answer to my dreams. She was a clone of

Janelle, but not my wife, and not addicted to high-powered management consulting.

Within one month my practice went from profitable to insanely lucrative. Janelle was paid well, and I was always making money, so by outward appearance our lifestyles did not alter much, but the financial changes were dramatic and fantastic. I went from making car payments to paying cash for cars. We went from deciding on when to remodel the kitchen to remodeling the kitchen and all three bathrooms for cash. We paid off our house in three years, just in time for Janelle to lose her job. I don't know if my cash flow was one of the causes of her breakdown. She said it didn't matter, but I have an aching suspicion that being flush with money despite losing her salary added to her sense of worthlessness.

"What can I do?" were the first words out of Danette's mouth. I had yet to ask her for anything. She answered the phone and spoke before I could get out my questions. I had left her a voicemail earlier that morning, calling her right after I hung up with the 911 operator, to let her know I was not going to be in for work.

If you have not made the connection, Daniel is a combination of Danette and Janelle, a nod to the two most important women in my life. Janelle let me pick the name in an effort to include me in the pregnancy. I selected the name during the third trimester, well before Daniel was born and I realized I wanted little to nothing to do with him.

"The FBI is here. They need our last two years of clients. Give me our summary profiles, employer, payment history. See if there are any early dismissals from the program due to money problems or loss of insurance. Can you print it out and fax it over? Maybe scan it and email?"

"Jesus, Gabriel." Danette used my full name. She said it added an air of prestige, Dr. Gabriel. "You know I can just create the document and send it. Print, scan, and email? Are you serious?" She stopped, realizing my mindset and the situation. "I'm sorry, that was rude. Absolutely, you'll have it in two minutes."

"Dani." I returned her lengthening of my name by calling her Dani. No one called her Dani, not even her parents when she was a little girl. She was Danette to all but me. "Don't worry about it. None of us know how to act right now. Just keep my office running. Call Stewart if you need help." Stewart Givens was my best friend in dentistry school. He worked for a large Orthodontics firm in town. He was a senior person at the office, and could probably duck out to help me if asked.

"I know you, Gabriel, so realize I say this with the best intentions, I often keep the office running despite you being here. Focus on Daniel and Janelle, do whatever you need to do, take all the time you need. I will make sure we don't skip a beat here, and I'll get the reports over immediately. I'll email the last two years, and do a quick scan for removals and bad payment histories in the last ten, though that covers the recession, so I'm not sure how helpful it will be."

"Thank you." I wanted to get back inside. "I'll keep you as up to date as possible. Gotta run." I turned around to find the older FBI man standing directly behind me. He was listening, though he pretended to be checking his email. He was one tall son of a bitch. I guessed he had four inches on me.

"Everything okay?" he asked smoothly.

"My practice manager is sending the reports now. She is also going to pull early removals and bad payment histories for the last ten years." I paused for a second. "Early removals are patients we take the braces off before their teeth are straightened or bites corrected, typically done for financial reasons."

The tall guy seemed to ignore me. "I need your employees' names. We'll be looking into each one of them." He flipped open a small pad of paper. "Who were you just speaking with?"

I so wanted to correct his grammar, "you mean with whom was I just speaking?" but I did not. He may have been weird and invasive, but he was trying to find Daniel. I was learning to tone down my asshole tendencies for the time being.

"Danette Sweets. She has been my practice manager for seven years. She worked with my wife before accepting the position with me. She is Daniel's godmother and accounts for the first half of his name."

He scribbled her name on the paper, nodding politely.

"And how many other people are in your office?"

I gave him the numbers. "Fifty full-time employees, twenty part-time, and five dental school interns. I also hire two high school girls per office to work in the afternoons. I say that I hire them, but Dani takes care of the offices. I'm the talent. I don't handle personnel issues. Let me send a note to Dani about getting me the employee list."

I opened the email on my phone, asking for the employee list, their addresses, salaries, and any information she could provide. I asked for her name and address to be included in the list.

The patient information was already posted to my inbox.

"And how well do you pay Danette?" the FBI man asked, prepared to write the number next to her name.

"I don't pay her a salary. We are partners. She takes home 40 percent of the practice profits. If something happens to me, if anything keeps me from working, Janelle takes over my 60 percent and they would hire another head orthodontist, presumably by cutting that person in on the profits. Dani is a bad suspect. Her situation only gets hurt if I leave the practice."

"How much did she make last year?"

"Dani took home around $650,000 last year." He wrote the number in his book, and I watched his eyes widen in amazement ever so slightly. He did have emotions, and I could shock him.

"Is that typical for an office manager?" I could not be sure, but I believe he was more curious about than needed this information to find Daniel.

"She is my practice manager, not an office manager. From what I gather speaking with peers, no, but I'm making three to four times what some of my peers make, not all of my peers, but most, so I'm guessing it's a successful partnership."

The FBI man's eyes—yes, I really should learn his name—began to wander, looking at the quality of my house, the craftsmanship of my patio, fireplace, and pizza oven. He noted the subtle hints of extreme wealth. A quick glance would reveal a modest house in an expensive neighborhood. Janelle and I never considered moving even when we could afford to upscale. We loved our house, our street, our neighbors. We could have afforded a larger home and yard, but we did not need it. Even with Janelle's misuse of our cash, we were still flush, partly because we did not ramp up our expenses to meet our revenues.

If you moved beyond a quick glance, you would begin to notice the high-end finishing and "extras" we had.

When Daniel was born, we converted our guest room into his nursery. Our four-bedroom house was more than adequate for our five-member family. Instead of increasing the size, we upgraded the quality of the home.

"I know your wife had an affair a few years ago. Is there anything I should know about you?" He looked down at me as he asked. I realized why he came outside to listen to my phone call. He was separating me from Janelle, giving me the opportunity to come clean with any unsavory facts in my life.

"I have never cheated on my wife." That was the truth. "I don't so much as flirt with other women." Also true. "And I have a hard time characterizing my wife's infidelity as an affair. She was a bottomed-out alcoholic and gambling addict. She was living on the streets and survived how she needed to. Is it a great story to tell our kids? No, but it wasn't an affair that she broke off."

"So this," and he looked at his notes, "Rondo fellow is not a former lover?"

"He's the father of Daniel. He gave Janelle a place to sleep a few nights a week during that time. For all the horrible things people say about Rondo, he was decent enough to take her in despite her situation. I hate the man, but I'm grateful he saved her life. I'm not sure Janelle would have made it on the streets during the winter." I prayed my lies were convincing. I was trying to come off as a rational guy, one who saw the good in that evil bastard. I was trying to convince FBI guy that I accepted the positives of the relationship between my wife and Daniel's biological father.

Even if tall FBI man did not buy what I was selling, I hoped that he did not sense my newly growing anger and that I was fairly certain I was going to kill Rondo when this was all over.

"I am not here to judge your wife. I want to know if you have a jealous husband or jilted lover I need to investigate. I know this is difficult, but realize my sole purpose is to find your son." Twenty minutes ago I would have corrected him by saying "my wife's son." Things had changed quickly in my life.

"I know, and I'm telling you the truth. I would be astonished if one of my employees did this or was involved. I do not have an enemy. I have not cheated on my wife. I haven't screwed over an old business partner or stolen clients from a rival business. My wife has been unemployed for years. She gambled, but we never went into debt. She always used our cash. She doesn't owe a bookie or a loan shark. The only people I think would do this are Rondo, his friends, or Rondo's parents."

"Let's go back inside and find a way to print this list." He opened my back door, holding it for me to enter through. He was tall enough for me to comfortably walk under his arm.

I had already printed the list. I may not be a technological expert, but I know how to print from my phone.

Janelle was in tears at the table.

"Are you okay?" I moved toward her.

"We need that list," the man repeated.

"I'm okay, Gabe, get them what they need. I'm okay." She wiped the tears from her face with a tissue wadded up in her hand. "I'm having trouble keeping it together, but I'll do whatever I need to do, and I'll do it without a drink."

I knew the promise of not drinking did not extend to us not finding Daniel. It was a double-edged comment. I took solace in the fact that Janelle acknowledged her alcoholism, and that she had it under control, but I was also reminded of the fact that I could not stop her from ruining her life. Daniel saved her, not me, not the twins, not the life the four of us had before Daniel. I wondered if the twins thought about it, that their mother came back because of their new brother. I'm sure they were just happy to have her home, ecstatic that she was back in their lives, but maybe just a small part of them wondered why they weren't enough. Why she needed something else, a new son, to bring her back from the darkness. Did they ever feel inadequate because of it, like their love is worth less than Daniel's?

Or was that just me?

What can I say? I'm working through it.

I maintained eye contact with Janelle, turning the corners of my mouth up in a weak smile, a small gesture of love, something to connect us, to let her know I was with her. She returned my stare, dabbing the corners of her eyes again.

It was then I decided, no matter what it took, when this was over, I was going to kill Rondo.

Brad Manuel

I spent the next twenty minutes talking through my client list with Jerry, discussing any problem patients.

Jerry is the tall FBI guy. I finally looked at his badge and learned his name.

Here's the dirty little secret, if it's even a secret: I don't work on kids or adults who can't pay. Dani, when she came on board seven years ago, noticed that I always had a few delinquent payers on my client list, not many, but always a few. She plugged that leak immediately. We worked through the few remaining problem patients for three years, and the last four years have been filled with families who can afford my services.

It's little things like that, small business leaks that drag down the earning capacity of a practice. I'm an orthodontist, and regardless of how much business savvy I think I have, I do not have as much as a person who spent as much time learning business as I have learning orthodontics and dentistry. Most of my peers do not realize the power Dani brings to my office, or if they do, they do not have the access to a person of her caliber. The melding of quality orthodontic services with a superior business model has reaped tremendous financial rewards for both of us.

Consequently, I did not have any upset patients. I didn't have an upset parent, furious that I ripped the braces off their little girl for lack of payment. After twenty minutes scanning the two-year and ten-year patient list, Jerry and I acknowledged the names were likely a dead-end.

It was a dead-end for him, but for my side project with Janelle? The list brought me seven names, guards at the detention center holding Randall James Rondo as he awaited trial for armed robbery and assault with a deadly weapon.

Eighteen months ago, just about a week before Daniel was born, Randall Rondo was arrested for trying to rob a bar. The bartender was shot, surviving his wounds and fingering R.J. Rondo as the shooter. Video cameras confirmed the bartender's story. Rondo claimed the man owed him money and that he was not stealing, just taking what was due to him. He also said the shot fired was in self-defense against the shotgun Rondo knew was behind the counter. Unfortunately for Rondo, the video, lacking audio to confirm a conversation Rondo claimed happened before he fired, disputed his account of the evening.

The sire of my wife's child was looking at a long time in prison. Until his exact sentence was meted out, he spent his days in the Hamilton County Detention Facility.

I began to formulate a strategy in my head. How was this going to work? "Hello, Denise? This is Gabe Addison, your son's orthodontist. I am calling to ask if you will inquire with one of your prisoners, ask him if his family has kidnapped my son."

That did not seem like a winning strategy, but I'll be honest, I could not think of an alternative. Maybe playing the wounded, desperate father card was the right way to go. Regardless, I needed to get away from Jerry the FBI Guy for a few minutes to implement my weak and prone-to-failure plan. Even if the prison guard refused my request, who is going to blame me for asking?

Jerrod Mathias, a guard at Hamilton County, a father of five children, three of whom had been through my office with a fourth currently wearing my braces, was my first phone call.

"Jerry." I was on a first name basis with my new best friend the FBI guy. "I really want to make some calls to family, let them know what his happening, assemble the troops if you will." I used a somber voice. "The Amber Alert is out, the news is scrolling, I can't let Janelle's parents see it without calling first. I can't let my family find out from the news. We've been with the police or you for hours."

Jerry nodded. He displayed the tiniest amount of emotion; I would almost call it sympathy. "Sure, Dr. Addison." I guess we weren't as close as I believed. He didn't call me Gabe. "Take a few minutes. Ask them if they have any ideas, might have noticed something when they were here, anything that can help us find your son." Jerry would not use Daniel's name. He dehumanized him by saying "your son." If my job were to find missing children, I guess I would find coping mechanisms too.

"Thank you." I gave him the customary respect and gratitude. I measured my movements, making sure to not seem anxious or hurried. I walked down the hall, turned the corner, trudged up the stairs, and made it to my bedroom. I shut the door, listened for following footsteps, and when I did not hear any, went through another door into my master bathroom.

I pulled up the patient information, found Jerrod Mathias's cell number, sat on my toilet, and called a man I barely knew, had probably never met, to ask him the tiny favor of questioning Randall James Rondo.

"Jerry Mathias," he answered after three rings.

Another Jerry? I was horrible with names, having as many men with the same one was a positive in an otherwise crappy situation.

"Jerry, if I may call you Jerry, this is Gabe Addison. I'm your family's orthodontist." Oh, my god, did that sound ridiculous.

"Sure, Dr. Addison, how can I help you? Is something wrong with Bryson's teeth? I'll be honest, my wife handles all of the braces stuff." A normal response to my call.

"Well, um." Really projecting strength, Gabe, stammering is such a sign of confidence. "Jerry, I am going to be blunt. This call isn't about Bryson. My eighteen-month-old son has been kidnapped."

"Jesus, I'm sorry." He was sincere and appeared to be a normal person giving normal responses to a random call from his kids' orthodontist.

"Yeah, well, the child is actually the biological son of one of the inmates at the Hamilton Detention Center. The FBI is here at my house, and they are at his family's house, but I am hoping, begging actually, to see if you might give this man a visit to see if he knows anything, ask him, well, with a strong arm and off the record."

I paused. Mr. Jerrod Mathias did not respond. A silence hung over the airwaves between our cell phones.

"I'm sorry I called. I am out of line. It's just that I'm so damn desperate." It was time to start covering my ass. "Forget I asked."

"Hold on." There was silence for another few seconds. "Sorry, I was moving into a private room." More silence. "What's the guy's name?"

Seriously? This was going to work? That was impossible, literally, impossible that my first attempt at reaching out to a guard was going to work.

"Randall Rondo," I replied quickly.

"Is this the best number to call back?" Jerry's tone was all business.

"It is."

"I work noon to midnight. I'll call you later today, when I've had a chance to speak with him."

That was it, the line went dead. I pulled the cell phone from my ear. The call time was stopped and blinking. I sat on my toilet staring at the digital numbers as they flashed.

I used my thumb to switch to my contacts list, dialed my brother, and began to explain the day. I followed up with calls to Janelle's parents, as well as other immediate family and friends. At one point I heard footsteps. I saw a set of black leather toes outside of the bathroom door. The door bottom was an inch off the newly installed hardwood, left high from the carpet we pulled out when we remodeled.

Seriously, who puts carpet in a bathroom? The new water-sealed reclaimed wood worked much better.

The leather wingtips waited, listening to my conversation. After a minute or so they spun around and left.

I made three more calls before I left the bathroom and went downstairs.

Janelle sat at the kitchen table talking on the phone. Our house was empty. I looked out the front storm door and saw six police officers in a circle. Three cruisers lined the street in front of the house. I went back to the kitchen to sit next to my wife.

"Gabe is back. We'll let you know what's happening." Pause. "I love you too."

Janelle put the phone on the table.

We stared at each other. I reached out and took her hand.

"I know they love him, and they are caring for him, so I don't think he's in trouble," she stated flatly. "But he's our son, and we are going to get him back. The pain I feel is not worry for Daniel, it's the fear I won't see him again."

"I know."

"But I am going to see him again. I know that. I believe that with all of my heart. The tears are gone until I hold him again. It's time to be strong."

"I know." I actually didn't know, didn't believe I could be strong enough to handle what needed to be done, but I faked it for now.

She gave me a moment. As I already mentioned, Janelle knows me. She can see what's happening in my head, the wheels spinning, the doubt I had about delving into the world she inhabited for a few months.

"You can do this, Gabe. We can do this. I know I've asked too much from you already. You've given me more love and support, put up with more crap." She waited for a moment. It was not a dramatic pause, or the pause of someone trying to manipulate me. We were done with manipulating, with lying, with cheating, with stealing. She was genuinely flummoxed with how to express her thoughts.

"You're damn right I have." I laughed. "But that's not what this is about."

She gave me a smile, a real smile, a grin of lightness and happiness.

"J, you know I've been sleepwalking through Daniel's life, going through the motions, treating him like a stepchild from a Grimm fairy tale. I can't apologize for it, because, well, that's just a stupid thing to say at the moment, like we are suddenly airing issues we both know are there." I took a breath. "I love you enough to take Daniel into my house, to let you raise him, but I know it's not enough. I get it. The good that will to come out of this insanity is that I'm all in, both feet, 100 percent. We are a family, no partial members. The boys love him. I love him. We get him back, whatever it takes, and we move forward."

She had the look in her eyes, one that I hope you have experienced. I can't put it into words, the love that emanated from her eyes, her face, her body. I'm sure she sees it from me. If I'd never seen the look before, I never would have taken her back, but I have seen it, and continue to see it.

She loves me.

"So where are we then?" she asked.

"I spoke to a guard. He is calling me back this afternoon. It was all pretty casual. I explained our situation. He told me he'd talk to Rondo."

"That's it?" she asked.

"That's what I thought. We'll see. I know, forty-eight hours before our son is in the wind." I needed some water. Three cups of coffee with no other liquid was giving me a dehydration headache. As I stood, my stomach growled. "Am I allowed to feed myself, or does that appear like I am guilty or uninterested?"

"I think you can eat." She remained at the table. "What did Danette say? All fine at the office? Did she have any insight?"

"Apparently, aside from the recession, we don't have any delinquents." I was mildly surprised as I relayed the news.

"Of course you don't. Danette isn't going to allow risky payers. She probably doesn't allow questionable personalities either." Janelle admired her old business associate's solid practice management.

"You and I know it isn't an angry customer or revenge-minded employee. This is Rondo's family, plain and simple." I placed a store-bought bagel in the toaster. I did not care for them, but my kids liked the speedy aspect of the tasteless doughy breads. I opened the cupboard and pulled out peanut butter to spread on my late breakfast.

"I sincerely hope it is him. That's the easiest resolution for us." She sipped a glass of orange juice acquired while I was in the bathroom on the phone. "My fear is it isn't him or his family. Then we are truly in the dark."

"Who else could it be? A random?" The toaster popped up, and I grabbed my bagel. "Seriously, J, that doesn't make sense. Who is going to randomly come into our security-monitored house and steal our baby? Not even a baby, a damn toddler? It has to be them."

I looked at her sitting at the table sipping her orange juice. She had doubt.

"I hope we're right. It will be so damn easy if we are right."

If? What did she mean if?

We were on our way to a Midwest FBI field office. Police cruisers escorted us in front and behind as we drove a quick route to downtown Cincinnati.

My phone buzzed and I saw Stewart Givens's face on my phone. It was a goofy picture from a costume party at our country club. He wore a floppy plaid cap like an old-time golfer. A large pom-pom rested on top of the cap, and he had pasted thick, red sideburns on each cheek. A mustache connected the sideburns, running down his face a bit and back up over his mouth. It was his lame attempt at looking "Scottish."

If I haven't convinced you that I am not the man to run a search-and-rescue operation through the mean streets of Cincinnati, the fact that I have a country club costume party photo of my friend should drive the point home.

I pressed the answer button, putting him on speaker in the car.

"Stewart, hey, you're on speaker with me and Janelle." I feel it is polite to tell someone that they are on speakerphone and that there is a third party in the car. If my kids are in the car, I like to alert adult callers so they minimize their profanity.

"Let's play some golf!" he screamed, ignoring the information that he was on speakerphone. "Dude, it's gorgeous out. I'm on my way to the club. Meet me there. Janelle can take the car. I'll give you a ride home."

"Why aren't you at work?" Janelle asked suspiciously. She did not care for Stewart, though she tolerated him because Stewart was my one true friend from graduate school, and he predated her in my life.

"Running a little fever today, can't tighten brackets"

One of the rules of dentistry, don't work in someone's mouth when you are sick.

"But, hey, just because I'm hot doesn't mean I can't play golf. Teddy is out of town." Teddy is Stewart's wife. "If your beautiful wife will let you free for a few hours, we can grab nine or even eighteen." Stewart always complimented Janelle's appearance. I would say he was sucking up while on the car's speakerphone, but it did not matter if she was with me or not. He always referred to her as "your knockout bride" or "how's your hot wife?"

"Someone kidnapped Daniel last night. We are on our way to the FBI's office." I was not in a jovial mood.

"What the fuck are you talking about?" Stewart was one of the people I tried to minimize on speaker, particularly when my kids were in the car. He did not have a profanity filter. He and his wife did not or could not have children. I never asked him which; it was none of my business. With a lack of children, he never stopped talking like he was in the locker room.

"Yeah, don't have much else to say. We are trying to keep it together." Janelle put her hand on my leg, giving it a quick squeeze.

"Jesus." He paused. "Well." He was stuttering, trying to figure out what to say, maybe if he even should be saying anything. I'm not saying Stewart didn't understand because he didn't have kids, but, well, he didn't. I know that might sound mean or crass, that a friend of mine, a dear friend, who might not be capable of fathering children, and thus cannot grasp the desperation, anxiety, and sadness I was feeling because I'd just lost one of mine, but sometimes you just have to be honest, crass or not. That therapist was moving up in my eyes.

"Do you need help with the twins? Can I do anything? I'm on my way over. Shit, you must be out of your head. It's that bastard, Rondo, isn't it?" He was trying to say the right things, and I appreciated it. I also knew there was no way in hell I would let him take care of the twins. He was a great guy, first one I'd call to play golf, first one I'd call for help with patients, but the last one I'd call to help with my sons, unless Teddy was with him.

"We aren't home, Stew, we are on our way to the FBI. We're pretty sure it is the Rondos, but in case it's not, let us know if you hear anything." What he would hear, I didn't know. Unless Daniel was at the golf course, I doubted Stewart Givens was going to be much help, and that was fine. I was not expecting anything from him. He could not disappoint me in this situation. "I'm sure the FBI will be in touch with you shortly. You're one of my only friends in town, and, well, you're the only African-American I have in my life. They asked me several times, you know, because of Daniel, to name my friends, coworkers, employees, and your name is always at the top of the list."

"First of all, do whatever you need to do, say whatever you need to say to get Janelle's son back."

Son of a bitch, he said "Janelle's son." Why did he say that? Had I said it to him one too many times? Had I been calling Daniel "Janelle's son" all this time? I turned to my wife, and she stared straight ahead. The look on her face could only be described as similar to a person eating lemons. Her lips were pursed, and her eyes were furious.

Listening to Stewart made me realize how horrible a person I had become over the last few years, and it made me sick to my stomach.

Despite my lack of response, Stewart continued to ramble. "And second of all, there are plenty of other suspects, not just me. Your partner's husband is black. Two of your office managers are black." Stewart began to make some light, off-color jokes about the situation, about how he was influencing my life and bringing more African Americans into it. He seemed oblivious to the fact that I was not part of the conversation, and the reason for my silence was that his humor might be just a little inappropriate for the seriousness of the situation.

I tried to shut him out, but decided that ending the call was the best course of action.

"Stewart, hey, we are almost here. I'll let you know what you can do. We appreciate it." I just wanted him off the phone.

41

"Will do, and yeah, I'm at the club if they need me. Man, shit, okay. Good luck." The phone clicked dead. I could not be sure Stewart didn't throw the phone out of his car window to escape the seriousness of our situation. Stew Givens did not do drama.

"Good luck?" Janelle asked me. "Seriously?"

She was graciously avoiding the "Janelle's son" comment.

"J, he's never aged past the age of 23. If anything, he's reverted to the age of 19. Not having kids will do that to you. Think of how much money he and Teddy have, with nothing to do but buy personal submarines from online magazines, and that kind of stupid shit."

"Whatever. At least he still thinks I'm attractive." Janelle was not a huge Stewart Givens fan. As I'm sure you understand, just because a couple is blissfully happy in marriage does not mean they don't have separate friends, friends who are not the "favorite" of their spouse. Janelle didn't owe me anything from her time away a few years ago, not one little thing. I took her back, that's my deal. She didn't need to pretend to like Stewart out of some sort of obligation or debt for my forgiveness.

Now, when she was a management consultant? The dinner parties I had to attend? She owes me big time for that crap. She could complain all she wanted about Givens, but she knows I suffered plenty, eating steak with a bunch of pumped up assholes who never asked me a single question about myself and talked incessantly about how great they are. I take that back; sometimes they would ask me what I did for a living, and then they might pitch their services to me, but other than the self-interested sales questions, I don't think many of Janelle's former colleagues even knew I was an orthodontist.

"And if Daniel is in a sand trap on the eighth hole, I'm sure Stew-dawg will give us a call." Janelle's venom had to go somewhere. She loved calling Stewart "Stew-dawg," as if he was cool enough to warrant such a nickname. Stewart was a nice guy and had been a good friend, helping me out when I need coverage at my practice, but he was definitely not a "Stew-dawg."

"Hey, he offered to help, let's not lump on him too much." I should have let it go.

"He's an asshole. He is always staring at me, lets me know how pretty he thinks I am, and quite frankly, he's jealous of you, Gabe. He was a good friend a dozen years ago, but now that you've raced by him with your practice, your wife, your kids, he can't handle it."

There was truth to what she was saying. We'd been over it a million times. The recession hit orthodontics hard. Braces are a bit of a luxury. They are expensive, and most people need some kind of insurance to put them on. The downturn hit the industry from both sides. People lost their jobs, losing their insurance, and people with jobs cut back on luxury items. A lot of my friends, Stewart included, had to let dental assistants go, cut back on staff. Hell, some of my old classmates went under. I, by the basic luck of having partnered with Dani, thrived. She innovated our payment plans, scooped up patients from shuttered practices, offered closing orthodontists a percentage of the income if they handed over their client lists, and she kept our offices bustling. One of my favorite things she did? She upped our magazine subscriptions. She made sure people had current issues of top-end magazines to read. Children's magazines too. It set us apart, gave us the appearance of prosperity. Perception is often the key to success in a commoditized industry. I'm telling you, marrying top-of-the-line business with high-end orthodontics, incredible.

Stewart's practice did not go under entirely, but he was forced to sell it for peanuts to a huge Ortho-conglomerate, a McBraces if you will. I hired two of the dental assistants Stewart let go, great people who were top-notch, long-standing employees. He did not speak to me for months. I thought he would thank me for picking his trusted employees off the ground, but he was humiliated. It was in the late fall, early winter, when I hired his people. As soon as the tulips poked through the ground, and

Stewart needed a golfing partner, the bad feelings were set aside. He often said, "You have kids, I get it." Like I shoveled over his practice or stole his patients because I had to provide. I did neither. My mistake in our friendship was succeeding, over-exceeding, to be honest. I had the best practice. I had fun and happy kids. He helped me look for Janelle a few times, during the first months when I would drive around looking for her, before I let her go, and I could swear Stewart enjoyed helping me, not in a "I'm helping a friend way," but in a "I finally have one up on Gabe way."

Whatever, I thought, he was harmless, and he was not going to be part of our solution for finding Daniel.

I drove in silence after Janelle's blunt assessment of Stewart Givens.

"I'm sorry. I know he's your friend. I'm frustrated and lashing out. I mean, I am pretty hot, I can't blame him for telling the truth." Janelle's hand remained on my leg, and she gave me another squeeze.

"He's not going to be of any help, so, in his own words, fuck him." I turned with the lead police car. I was following them, as I had no earthly idea where the Cincinnati FBI field office was located.

If Janelle and I seemed less frantic than we should, more upset than worried, it was because, in our minds, we knew who had Daniel, and we knew Daniel was okay. He was with the Rondo family, people he actually knew, people he trusted, and people who were definitely taking care of him during the abduction. How else would he not make a sound when they took him last night? He had to know his kidnappers.

This was basically like the child abductions where the divorced parent has "stolen" the child and fled for another state.

Daniel's other parent was Randall Rondo, and he was a tough customer, living in and off of the fringe parts of Cincinnati. His family? They were a different story, and despite our differences, I would even go so far as to call them a wonderful group of people. His parents were hardworking, blue collar, and churchgoing. They had six children. Randall was the only one who was afoul of the law. I love that expression "afoul of the law." Anyway, they fought us for custody. It was not much of a fight. Janelle was the mother. Randall was in jail. We always offered visitation to the Rondo family, supervised, monitored, scheduled visitation, but visitation nonetheless. Even after the judge extended Janelle sole and full custody at the first hearing, we continued to allow visits. Despite us allowing access, the Rondos were relentless in their pursuit of legal, court-ordered shared custody of their first grandchild, fruitless and costly as it was to them.

It appeared, at least to us, that paying attorneys and counting on the legal system was not working, and instead of acknowledging their fate as grandparents, aunts, and uncles who were relegated to the sidelines because Daniel's father robbed and shot a man, the Rondo clan had decided to steal him from us.

"It doesn't make sense," Janelle said as we made another turn behind the police escort. "Why would they work inside of the law for so long, only to abandon it now?"

"Desperation," I responded. "Maybe they are out of money."

"Their church paid for the last two rounds. Money was always available. No, this is weird." Janelle threw her head back and stared out the sunroof. "Oh, my god, Gabe, what if it isn't them?"

"It's them, J. It has to be them. All the signs, clues, signals point to the Rondo family."

I was wrong, and I knew it as soon as we pulled into a parking lot with a beige sign reading "Federal Bureau of Investigation." That's when I saw them, the entire Rondo clan. The mother was in hysterics; her husband had his arm around her in an attempt to calm her down and comfort her. As we pulled up, I saw concern and panic on all of their faces.

Janelle jumped out of the car, and the old woman ran toward her. I was still in my driver's seat, but I heard the conversation, muffled as it was by the car.

"Who took our baby, Janelle? Who took that dear sweet baby?" It was hard not to hear Margaret Rondo. She was screaming, tears flowing down her face. "None of our fighting matters until we get that dear sweet boy back." She threw her arms around my wife.

My mouth dropped agape. I sat there catching flies for a few seconds as a new feeling swept over me. Remember how I said I knew what desperation was? I didn't.

Desperation was just starting.

I'll be honest, I don't remember most of the next hour.

I got out of the car. I was lightheaded. It was similar to the time I found our bank statements and saw that Janelle had used all of our vacation cash along with our living expenses. I did not know what she was using the money for, and I was stunned to see it gone.

Today I was woozy, stung by the realization that something very bad was happening. Up to this point I'd been treating Daniel's abduction with seriousness, but in the back of my mind there had been an "Ah, he's fine, those pesky Rondos took him. Darn them, we'll just find where they have Daniel and get him back."

Only the Rondos did not have Daniel.

As I stumbled toward Janelle and Margaret, I felt a hand on my shoulder. I turned to see Randall Rondo, the father, not the son. I often called him Randall Sr., but he was not a senior. He was Randall Tiberius Rondo, not Randall James Rondo.

"Are you okay, son?" He called me son as a term of endearment, I could tell. It was not the condescending tone he often used when he called me son. "Son, we are never going to stop fighting," or "Son, if you think this is over, you have no idea who you are speaking to."

"I was up to a second ago," I admitted.

He put his arms around me and whispered into my ear as if I were one of his sons. "We are family on this."

My mouth fell open just a little bit more. Randall Sr. just called me his family.

Again, I admit, I was lost for a little while, shaking hands with people I considered opponents for so long. Margaret Rondo held me in her arms for minutes, bouncing against me in loud sobs. She was a strong woman, raising six children while working as a schoolteacher. She put three through college, had two in college, and lost one child to a life of crime.

We commiserated, consoled, and compared notes in the parking lot for what seemed like forever. The tall FBI man and his partner watched from the doorway. Every so often I glanced at them, expecting a notepad in their hand as they scratched notes about what they were seeing, but none of that happened. It appeared as if they knew the Rondos were innocent, and that Janelle and I were innocent. This was a time to let the families grieve and merge into a single Daniel-seeking entity.

Janelle and I separated from the Rondos. We entered the FBI building and were placed in a holding lounge. It was not a cell or room like I'd seen in the movies. There wasn't a plain metal table with uncomfortable chairs. There was no large pane of mirrored glass. We were in comfortable leather chairs. There was a beautiful Persian rug on the floor. A couch stood along a wall, and another empty lounge chair was vacant next to the door.

Janelle was catatonic.

"Babe?" I offered. "J?"

She stared ahead, eyes not blinking. "I told you it was too perfect. I knew it wasn't them. I don't know why I let myself believe it was them. Maybe it was a coping mechanism. If it was the Rondos, then Daniel was safe, cared for, and I was going to get him back."

She turned her head. "I might never see him again, or worse, he might be dead already."

"He's not dead. Whoever took him had our security codes. They know our life. They knew our kids were gone." I was grasping at straws. "And just because Margaret and Randall Sr. don't have him does not mean Rondo didn't arrange for Daniel to be taken."

"Gabe, have you spoken to Randy in the last year?" Janelle called him Randy sometimes. They were friends before he raped her. I think it made him easier to talk about, referring to him with the friend or family version of his name. She asked me because she would not know if I had spoken to Randall. She and I did not talk about him. Another item on the list of things I am working on. I promise.

"No."

"He's mixed up, that's for sure. He's not a great person sometimes. He shot that man in the video, but I believe it was an early strike against the shotgun attack. I know self-defense means imminent danger, and in Randy's mind, he thought he was going to get shot."

"Janelle, what's your point?"

"He wouldn't do this. He's not that kind of bad."

"Really?" I was up for a lot of things today, but listening to a Randall Rondo defense was not one of them. "He raped you while you were passed out or too drunk to fight. He takes advantage of you by giving you shelter, doesn't use a condom, gets you pregnant, and now he's not 'that' kind of bad? Bullshit."

"Okay," she replied, still monotone, as if she were dead inside. "I might be wrong, but explain this one. Why would he kidnap Daniel from jail? He's not getting out. No one in his family thinks he's walking on this one. None of his lawyers think he's walking. Why would he steal Daniel? His family is obviously not involved. He doesn't have a girlfriend anymore."

"Maybe he is lashing out at us, sticking it to you one more time, or maybe someone kidnapped Rondo's kid to get back at him? Could the motive be because of him even though he was not involved directly? Will you at least acknowledge that he might be the cause of all of this?"

We had turned on each other, not in an accusatory way, but the frustration of the moment, and her trying to exonerate the rapist dirtbag who fathered Daniel, had moved our unified front into an argument. I don't know if that is textbook, for the loving couple to suddenly point fingers or blame at different people, but that's what was happening. As we fell back into the world Janelle made when she was a drunk, we began to fight.

"I don't know." Janelle stared forward. "I don't know anything anymore. I don't know if I'm ever going to see my baby again, and if I do, I don't know if he'll be breathing."

"Goddamn it." I stood and went to the door. I didn't want to fight with Janelle anymore. "What the hell is taking so long?" We had been sitting in the lounge for a while. The FBI duo was focusing on the Rondo family, believing they had a connection to Janelle's missing child.

My cell phone buzzed. I looked down at the phone number and recognized it as the number I had dialed earlier, Jerrod Mathias'. The prison guard was calling me back.

"Hey, this is Jerry." His voice was curt and serious.

"Yes."

"Your guy didn't do it. He confessed to a whole bunch of shit, but he didn't even know your son had been snatched. He looked scared when I told him."

"Scared?" I asked.

"Yeah, that's what I thought, so I asked him again, but with a little more force." Jerry had the phone close to his mouth, and his voice was loud and slightly muffled in my ear.

"Jesus, I don't want you to get in trouble."

Mathias started laughing. "I didn't lay a hand on your friend." He controlled himself. "Sorry, Doc, I know your son is missing. I don't mean to be light, but have you ever been in prison?"

"No."

"Ever been to a prison?"

"No, well, I took a tour once, was bidding on a state of Ohio contract to put braces on inmates."

"Well, this jail I work in? I don't have to touch Randall James Rondo to get him to talk. There are places I can threaten to send him. People I can threaten to let loose on him. He's not a big-time criminal, despite the attempted murder charge. He's a little fish in a real big ocean right now, and our water is pretty fuckin' deep. He's scared shitless, and he's gonna tell me just about anything I ask."

"Okay, so you just asked him if he took Daniel, and he said no, but you got the sense there was more to the story?" I was confused.

"First he said he was scared for his mother, who loves your kid. I thought that was bullshit, so I pressed him." Jerry's voice was full of pride. "And then he admitted there was a secret that he didn't want to get out. He didn't take the kid, and the secret was unrelated. Swear to God, he said 'unrelated.' That prison idiot is using his big words today."

"Did you ask him the secret?" I asked with hope.

"It's not his kid."

I almost dropped the phone.

"That's a lie. He raped my wife." I raised my voice slightly, anger bubbling in my throat.

"He said he never slept with your lady, that he had a girlfriend that was really jealous and never left him alone with Jan. I assume that's your wife." Rondo liked calling Janelle Jan. She hated the name Jan, corrected anyone who called her that. I believed she went by that horrible shortened name while she was away so it seemed like she was a different person. She wasn't Janelle or J, she was Jan. "He said some guy used to come around and pay him to screw her. He didn't know who he was, just some guy who always seemed to know when she was too drunk to realize, or passed out, which I guess was all the time according to Randall. The mystery guy paid a couple of hundred bucks for Randall to leave the room."

I had no response. I was literally struck dumb.

"Doc?" I'd never been called Doc. I kind of liked it. It made me feel like I was in the army, on the battlefield, and people were screaming, "Doc!" It gave me more importance and prestige than I deserved or had ever had before.

"Doc," Jerry said one more time. "Hey, I gotta run. The FBI has a woman here, and the police have Randall in a cell. I don't know if he's going to tell them anything. I would bet not, but you never know. If I had to guess, you, me, and Randall are the only ones who know it ain't his kid."

I had nothing to say.

"Look, I'm sorry I didn't find your son, but maybe this will help you look somewhere else." He waited for me to respond.

"Thank you, Jerry."

"Glad to help, Doc."

It was my turn to be a stereotypical movie character, staring at a phone after bad news. Dumbfounded by a plot twist, and this was a gigantic plot twist. Not only did Randall not take our son, but he wasn't the father. I'd never have to see or deal with the Rondos again. All I needed to do was ask him to establish paternity at the next hearing. Done, gone, out of my life.

But as they say, the devil you know…

Rondo was going to jail for decades. His family was loving and kind. I would not say he was my ideal choice for the father of my son, but knowing my wife didn't have the foggiest idea who the actual father was? Knowing my wife didn't even know there was another guy?

"What did he say?" Janelle was touching my arm. She was out of her chair, out of her catatonic state. She had some color in her face, hope that I was about to solve her problems.

"He said it isn't Rondo. Randall is just as panicked as we are, scared for his mother or something like that." I hoped I was as good at lying as my wife. "We are at a dead-end with the Rondos. It's time I start to follow your old paths, find out what enemies you might have made, or who might be reaching out from that time to take advantage of us."

Janelle nodded. She walked to a small coffee table, picked up a pencil and notepad, and started scribbling. "They are going to search our phones, texts, and email. I know this is hilariously ironic, but I think we should write all of our stuff on paper, make hard copies we can destroy with fire. The electronic trail is too easy to trace."

"Should I turn off my phone?" The phone was a beacon for the FBI to follow me.

"No, just slip it into my purse or jacket pocket. We'll say you left it on the table and I picked it up." She finished writing and handed me a list of three addresses. "Here are the gambling places I used. One is a card game in Mount Adams. I was not up to speed and lost too much even for my self-destructive ambitions. I stuck to the ponies and some of the other options here." She pointed to an address in Oakley. Both of the neighborhoods she spoke of were high-end. They were not as tony as where we lived, but they were not poor, dangerous parts of town.

"How the hell did you find a gambling spot in Mount Adams?"

"They want customers, Gabe. They go where people feel comfortable. You think they can get high rollers if all of the games are Over-the-Rhine?" Over-the-Rhine is a poor, dangerous neighborhood, and more in line with where I assumed a gambling ring would be. "I ended up with Randy in Walnut Hills, but when I started? I went to these places." She moved her finger back to the address in Oakley. "This one was the nicest of the 'seedy' places. I would usually finish my nights in Walnut Hills. That's were Rondo lived. Sometimes I'd be in Corryville for the night. It depended on how drunk I was." Corryville was near the University of Cincinnati. Walnut Hills was the next neighborhood over from where we lived in Hyde Park, but it was light-years away in income. It had pockets of nice homes, but pockets of despair too.

"I'll wait until after dark." I replied.

Janelle laughed. "Gabe, they run all day. If you can sneak out of here, you can go right now." She wore a smile as she shook her head. "I went by Jan. I wrote the names of the managers of each place. They'll remember me. I was an unusual client. There are not many women who dressed and looked like me, at least when I started. By the end, I was just another washed-out drunk."

I'd never heard Janelle speak of herself so negatively. Her voice, at least for the last sentence, had a tone of derision. We spoke of her gambling little, maybe in therapy, but dwelling on the specifics was never productive. We focused on the big picture, the "us" part of the relationship. I knew Janelle looked at that time as a failed attempt to destroy herself. She is Type A in the purest sense, and poured all of her drive and talent into ruining her life. Daniel thwarted the efforts.

I wonder if she considered herself a failure at failing.

"You think I can just leave?" I held my phone out to her.

She nodded. "What are they going to do? Arrest you? What father is going to sit around and do nothing? I say you take matters into your own hands. Walk out the door."

I contemplated the move. If I left, I would create suspicion. Hell, the FBI might even follow me, but would that be the worst thing? We wanted them to find Daniel. If following me got them out of the office and to the right locations, that was a benefit.

Leaving also meant I was less likely to tell Janelle that Rondo was not Daniel's father.

I hugged her and kissed her firmly on the lips.

"I love you."

I turned and went out the open door. I asked a gray-suited woman sitting at a desk about the bathroom. She pointed toward a hallway. Luck was on my side; it was the same hallway as the stairway to freedom.

No alarms sounded. No rush of people came out of the door after me. I used the bathroom, not knowing when I would see a clean one again, took a left instead of a right when I exited, walked down two flights of stairs to my car, and I was free.

I pulled out of the parking lot quickly, and headed toward Mount Adams, a neighborhood I knew well from my youthful drinking days with Stewart Givens.

The first address on the small sheet of paper I held was a building on the edge of Mount Adams, almost touching the adjacent neighborhood of Walnut Hills. That made sense to me. As I've already explained Walnut Hills is a neighborhood with pockets of poverty and despair. Still, this address was firmly on the Mount Adams side of the tracks. Actually, I could have sworn that I'd been to a party in an apartment there. It was a six-story, gray stucco that screamed apartment building. There were thousands of these scattered all around Cincinnati. The obligatory balconies dotted the side, a standard bulkhead separating the outdoor spaces from each other.

The note Janelle left for me on the piece of paper read, "Apartment 312, ask for Phil." The instructions were plain and direct, but I was worried they were too vague. What kind of place was this? I'm an orthodontist, had she forgotten? Was it as simple as knocking on a door and asking for the right guy?

I looked at the paper again, turning it over in hopes I would find an additional paragraph of instructions. There was nothing. The brief notes were written in Janelle's perfect handwriting. Dani had similar penmanship, perfect, clear, legible. If medical professions taught poor handwriting, management consulting firms went the other way. I'm sure it is drilled into their heads, "you represent the firm, clients are paying you a lot of money, write like an adult…"

I took a deep breath and walked toward the building. There was a brass panel with dozens of white buttons, similar to an array of doorbells, on the outside of the glass door to the lobby. I tried the door, but it was locked. Most of the buzzers had a last name next to them, like "Mitchell," written in blue ballpoint or black marker on a white sticker, obviously pasted over the previous occupant's sticker. The buzzer next to 312 was not marked with a name. I could see the remnants of an old sticker.

I pressed the button and waited.

I looked around for a camera but could not identify one. I doubted a building this old would provide a camera for the apartment dwellers. Regardless, I was suddenly self-conscious about my clothes. I'd dressed for a day at the FBI, possibly a television interview. My golf shirt and linen pants were perfect for a nice lunch, but a gambling hall? At least I'd left my sweater in the car.

"Yeah." A gruff voice sang through the low-quality speaker, crackles and pops accompanying the greeting.

I pressed the button to respond. "My name is Gabe Addison. My wife, Janelle, used to come here. She told me to ask for Phil." I released the button and waited.

"Hey, asshole, the button is a buzzer, which you just pressed for ten seconds. Just talk into the speaker, dumbass."

"I, um, wow, sorry. My name is Gabe Addison."

"Congrats, fuck off and find someone else to bother."

I heard a final pop. "My wife, Janelle, sent me?"

The person was gone, that pop was him terminating the connection.

I pressed the buzzer.

"Hey, asshole, you are about to be very unhappy."

"Janelle sent me, told me to ask for Phil." I caught myself. "Jan sent me. You probably know her as Jan."

There wasn't a pop from the box's speaker this time. The angry person received my last message.

The door buzzed. I pulled it open and made my way up to 312.

The door was open a crack, and I heard a low sound of voices with an occasional spike of laughter. I pushed the door open and entered an apartment. A very heavy, I'll go so far as to call him fat, man sat on a chair reading *The Economist*. I wish I was clever enough to make that up. He was reading the damn *Economist*. It was a tall chair, probably from a high-top table or kitchen lunch counter.

"You don't smoke, do you?" he asked through the magazine, not looking up at me to make eye contact.

"No." I was playing it cool, responding when spoken to, using the minimum number of words and information in my answers.

"Good, 'cause Phil's mom found a spot on her lung last year, and he don't let no one smoke no more. No exceptions, and cigars are smoking, so don't try that bullshit neither."

He dropped the top of the magazine to give me a scan. "Shit." He chuckled. "Jan sent you? You do something bad to her?" He stopped laughing for a second. "Cash only, and I hope you brought a shit-ton."

"I'm her husband. Our son was kidnapped this morning. She sent me here to ask if you know anything or, I guess, if Phil knows anything."

"I'm sorry." He stood up from the tall chair. "But your kid ain't here."

The man was monstrous in size, fat and tall. He was using the high-top chair because he obviously, because of his height, could not fit comfortably in a regular one. I've met a few of the local NFL players, linemen, and this man was the same build.

"Jan sent me here to talk to Phil. Maybe I can ask him a question? I don't want any trouble." I doubted I could cause any trouble, and I knew this guy was not worried about trouble from me. It was a statement to show I knew my place, my position of weakness.

"Buddy, you could never cause trouble." See? He knew I was a nothing. "And missing kid or not, you ain't getting back into the game without $2,500. That's the buy-in. I'll even go so far as to tell you the truth, I got no idea who the fuck Jan is, but Phil is a name I know. You want to see him, you know the price." He gave me one more look before sitting back on his chair and putting his magazine in front of his face.

"Seriously, I don't want to play, I just want to ask Phil about my missing son." I made a turn toward a hallway in the apartment where I heard voices. I mean, surely this guy was going to let me ask a quick question. Who wouldn't let me ask a question? He knew I was not a threat.

When my back was fully turned, but before I could take a step, an enormous hand wrapped around my upper left arm. It squeezed tightly, sending pain throughout my entire body. My knees buckled, and I could swear I almost blacked out.

"I'm not a nice guy." The giant man's mouth was right next to my ear. He was holding me up as my body sagged. My shoulder felt like it was dislocating from the weight of a worthless body. He was holding me upright, my left shoulder sticking in the air. "But I have a kid, so I am going to be nice." His hand squeezed around my arm with more force, which seemed impossible as I already had little to no feeling in my hand. "Normally I would beat you, badly. If you get $2,500, I will let you buy into the game, but if you don't have the money, don't come back."

He let go of my arm, and I crumpled to the floor. My breathing was labored, and my heart was racing. The encounter was less than ten seconds, but I was soaked with sweat.

"I—" That was all I could muster, a meek one word, begging for something.

The exchange was over for the fat guy. He was back to reading his magazine.

I could not feel my left arm. It dangled uselessly. I was on the floor in what should have been an "all fours" position, but I could only use three limbs. I pushed my body up with my one good arm and walked out of the door, leaving it ajar as when I entered.

I did not hesitate, walking briskly to the stairs, pushing open the door, and standing in the well for a few seconds. My breath was still coming quickly, and I threw up. I tried to contain the vomit to the corner behind the door. Some of it splashed onto my shoes. It was early in the afternoon, and no one was around to witness my party foul. This was an apartment building in a neighborhood of young professionals, working long hours. In theory no one would see my barf until well after 5 p.m.

It took me a few minutes to collect myself. I'm almost positive I cried. There were definitely whimpers and heavy intakes with my lower lip sucking in and out. That was the first time I had been struck or touched in a negative manner since grade school, and honestly, I'm not sure I was in a fight back then either. If I am totally honest, I think that is the first time I had submitted, physically, to another person because of the threat of personal violence.

The feeling was devastating. I was terrified to my core. The safe, happy, protective bubble I had lived in my entire life was gone. The fat man with the vise grip, who had so quickly and easily dismantled me, had no fear of repercussion. He wasn't afraid of me physically. He knew I did not have the courage to bring a gun. He obviously did not fear the police. He probably figured out pretty quickly I was working outside of the police anyway. Why would a country club-dressed man show up looking for a kid without the police?

I was so far outside of my comfort zone, I did not know how to feel. His words rang in my ears. "I'm not a nice guy." "Normally I would beat you, badly." He was holding back because he was a father. That was the only thing saving me from the emergency room.

That was it. I was done. My left arm hung limply, throbbing with pain. My forehead was leaning against my right forearm, which was resting on the wall. I got my breathing under control, wanting to leave this stairwell as the stench of vomit took over the air.

My entire time in the building was probably a little over ten minutes, certainly no longer than fifteen. In that short span I had gone from a relatively confident, definitely successful orthodontist, to a man with one arm, the taste of throw up in his mouth, and the fear of God.

"I'll go back to the FBI, let them handle this," I said in my head as I marched slowly down the stairs to the first floor. "I am out of my league. This is too dangerous." The decision was made. I would drive back to my house, brush my teeth, change my shoes, and go back to the FBI field office.

But instead of that, instead of doing the sensible thing, I made my way to my car and drove to my local bank branch to take out $2,500.

The numbness in my arm subsided, replaced by an angry, blood-pumping, painful throb. My head also cleared, and I thought about my plan. I found some gum in the armrest, stuffed two pieces of mint into my mouth to clear the puke taste, and sat in the bank parking lot. If Phil's card game was the highest stakes game, and it was $2,500, if and when I traveled downstream to visit seedier places, I'd also need cash.

How much could I ask for at the bank? I certainly had enough money to cover a large withdrawal, but when did the police get summoned? I did not know these things, had only heard rumors that the government had levels in place to identify drug dealers or other nefarious characters operating in cash to avoid suspicion or, more to the point, taxes.

I was sweating when I asked the teller for $5,000. I hoped that was more than enough to follow the life of my wife's alter ego, Jan, and I hoped it was an amount that did not raise suspicion.

Like many times in life when you think eyes are watching you or it might be a big deal, neither was the case. As I said, I have the money to extract $5,000. I had a driver's license. I had an ATM card. I had the PIN code. I actually think the teller was bored as she counted the fifties and hundreds.

"Have a nice day, Mr. Addison."

"You too." I smiled, grimacing as I lowered my left arm from the high counter. I had placed it there in an effort to appear casual.

I asked for two envelopes. One contained $2,500 in hundred dollar bills. The other envelope had $2,500 in fifties. I slipped the money into my pants pocket and went back to my car.

I sat in the driver's seat holding onto the steering wheel and working through some breathing exercises to calm my heart and head. After a minute of "in through the nose, out through the mouth," I felt as ready as possible. I pulled the envelopes of money from my pocket. I identified the hundreds and placed that white packet back in my pocket. I took

$300 from the fifties envelope and placed the money in my wallet. I put the rest of that cash under my seat in case I needed it later.

I took another thirty seconds to breathe and drove back to the apartment building.

The same gruff voice greeted my press of the 312 buzzer.

"Yeah."

"I'm back."

The lock on the door clicked, and I walked back into the lion's den.

The apartment door was still open, and I pushed it to accommodate my entry into the living room. I made sure not to shut the door behind me, leaving the crack.

"You can shut it." The big man told me from the stool/chair. "I open it when I buzz people up."

I obeyed and closed the door completely, gulping a bit when I heard the lock click.

"I'm guessing you brought the money."

I pulled the envelope from my pocket and extended my hand to him.

"Give me $200. You use the rest to buy into the game."

I obeyed his command, pulling two one hundred dollar bills from the white packet. He accepted the money and got off his chair.

I followed him as he walked toward the voices coming from the other rooms of the apartment.

It was a one-bedroom condo. The short "hallway" was an inset. A bathroom was on the left, and a bedroom was on the right. The bedroom contained a large, black felt-covered poker table. A single sofa stood against one wall. A woman, scantily clad as my mother would say, sat on the couch looking at her phone.

Six people sat around the table. A hand was dealt, and the conversation from a moment ago was gone as the players examined their cards.

I stood quietly. I was scared, terrified really. The enormous man had already proved he could debilitate me with a single squeeze of his hand. I did not want to see what he would do if told to punish me for speaking out of turn. It was an odd sensation, this feeling of fear and helplessness. I should have been examining the room, looking at the six people to figure out which one was Phil. I should have looked to see if one of them was

Jan's rapist, maybe Daniel's kidnapper, but instead I stood frozen with fear, paralyzed by the still pulsing pain in my arm.

You know what I thought about? I thought about Randall James Rondo talking to my prison guard friend Jerry and how Rondo probably felt the same way. Jerry referred to the ability to "send" Rondo places, unleash other inmates upon him. I wondered if Randall broke his two-year secret to Jerry because he felt the exact same way I felt now, helpless, scared, and naked.

At that moment, for a brief second, I felt pity for Rondo. I might go so far as to say I had empathy. How bizarre a feeling, to have empathy for a man who whored out my wife when she was drunk, who put his family through hell by lying about the paternity of our son, yet I had it. I had that sliver of feeling, like a man whose neck is stretched across a log, waiting to be chopped off, and he thinks, "I wonder how this affects the executioner. That poor axe-wielding man has to live with these deaths day in and day out."

Okay, maybe not that extreme an analogy, but close.

"Hey, Chi Chi, you gonna sit down or what?"

Someone was speaking to me. I was completely zoned out.

"What?" was my only logical response. He was calling me "Chi Chi" as a reference to Chi Chi Rodriguez, a famous golfer, making a joke about my attire.

"I hope he brought a lot of money, because he's either the best card player in the world, or we all just got a little richer. I'm betting the latter." A woman in a teal track suit laughed after her comment. She was older with gray, curly hair. She was not Phil, so I ignored her.

"Joe?" A thin man in a yellow golf shirt, the same brand as the shirt I was wearing in fact, looked past me to the large man from the other room.

"He has money, Phil. Said Jan sent him." The guard elephant's name was Joe. Good to know.

"Who is Jan?" Phil asked the room, looking back and forth across the table.

I spoke. My voice was a little shaky, but I managed to get out. "Jan is my wife. She told me she played here a few years ago. She's a brunette woman, attractive, drank too much." I assumed she drank too much.

"You just described most of the women who walk through that door, buddy." Phil flipped his head back in a gesture to Joe. I felt a heavy hand land on my collarbone.

"Wait, wait, please, our son was kidnapped this morning. Jan used to come here when she was drinking. Do you know any African-American players who like to rape women? Maybe followed her?"

Phil put his hand in the air signaling Joe to stop his forcible removal of my body. "Joe, hold on a sec." Phil stood. He was a thin man, maybe in his late fifties. His biceps were muscular, and his chin was chiseled. I could tell he worked out, a lot. I was surprised, as I expected a stereotypical mob boss, basically a fat man. He looked like a personal trainer and dressed like one too. He wore the aforementioned yellow golf shirt with blue nylon track pants.

Phil was my height, maybe five foot ten inches. He was not a physically intimidating person, yet Joe released my collar bone immediately. The giant even took a step back.

"Let me get this straight," Phil began. I noticed the other people in the room averted their eyes, staring down at the table or grabbing their phones. No one wanted to draw Phil's ire away from me.

I felt sweat begin to form on my back, forehead, and underarms.

"Your son gets kidnapped, and you come here looking for the culprit?" He walked from the other side of the table toward me. My mind raced.

Could I make it out of this apartment without being caught? Did I have a chance to push Joe out of my way? Should I have assumed the man sitting directly across from the door was Phil? What mistakes had I made?

"Phil, I'm desperate. My wife used to play here. She gave me the address, told me your name. I'm not here with the police or FBI. I'm a father looking for his child."

No one offered me assistance. I thought I might get a "come on, Phil, let the guy off."

"Tell you what," he told me when he paused a few inches from my face. "Joe already hurt you pretty good, and you came back, so I'll give you the benefit of the doubt that what you say is true." He stopped for a second, staring straight into my eyes. He had no fear, just like I said about Joe earlier. There were no ramifications for Phil's actions. Phil did what Phil wanted to do. He might go to jail, he might get killed by some up-and-comer, but those were outcomes out of his control. The true reason to be scared of him was, in the brief moment I locked eyes with the man, I could tell there were no moral conflicts in his mind. Phil lived like a shark, pure and simple. He did what he did, no regrets, no consequences, and probably no hesitation. He swam through life eating whatever the hell he wanted to eat. Joe was big, strong, maybe fearless, but he had a sliver of a conscience.

Phil could have shot me dead and sat back down at the table to deal the cards.

"I am going to let you walk out of here after you give me $2,000. I don't want to see you ever again, and I am not going to answer your questions."

"Please, if you have any idea who might have taken my son." I was reading Phil for the first time. He was not going to kill me. I still wasn't sure if he was going to hurt me or have Joe hurt me, but I was going to make it out of the apartment alive. I decided to take a final shot at getting information.

"How do you think my patrons would react to me giving you names? Do you think these five great people would take kindly to me telling you about past members of my little group? Do you think it would be a good business move for me to talk to you, have word get around that I snitch?" Phil was still an inch from my face. He displayed no emotion. His voice was calm and even. He was almost soothing in his reply, speaking with common sense from the most logical position.

"I guess not," I replied finally.

"You guess not," he told me. "How about you give me the money, take a walk back out to your car, and let us get back to our game? Does that also sound reasonable to you?"

I heard a few chuckles from the table. I understood the humor, though I was not in a joking mood. Instead, I nodded, dropped my eyes from his, took a step back, and turned to walk out of the room.

"I'm sorry to have bothered you," I said weakly, humiliated with cowardice as I reached into my pocket.

"Not here," Phil instructed me. "I'll take the money out there." He did not take his eyes off of me, but he spoke to the room. "I just won my next pot. You play a hand without me."

I heard cards being shuffled as Phil's arm went across my shoulders to escort me out of the room. Joe fell in line behind us.

As soon as we were to the small kitchen counter in the outer room, I pulled the white envelope of bills from my pocket. I pulled three hundreds out of it and stuffed them in my pocket.

Phil accepted the money, pulling the bills from the packet to count them. It was not a difficult task, counting twenty-one hundred dollar bills. He spoke to me at the same time.

"I don't have any idea who took your kid." He kept his head down. "I'm not just saying that. I don't know. I don't remember your wife. I get a lot

of patsies in here, rich drunks that I shear and let back into the pasture."
The man had an intellect and a keen sense of metaphors. "I try not to
judge people too much, you know. People live how they're gonna live."
Phil was finished counting. He folded the money and placed it in his pants
pocket. "But nobody likes a pedophile, and I don't play cards with
kidnappers."

He did not nod, he looked straight at me. It must have been his thing, to
bore into a person's soul with his piercing, remorseless, terrifying, shark
like eyes. He gave me the look for a second, maybe two, and then he
turned around and went back to the game.

"Thanks," I said to Phil before he was more than a step away. He did not
acknowledge my gratitude.

Joe was back in his seat, *The Economist* in hand. "You still here?" he
asked me, indicating that I was close to being forcibly removed.

"I was just leaving." And I did, as fast as I could.

I almost ran down the hall and was back in the vomit-filled stairwell
immediately. I took a moment to collect myself.

A young woman in hospital scrubs came up the stairs. She made a face
when she smelled and saw the throw up. I held the door open for her,
and we exchanged disgusted glances. Did she know about the game on
her hall? A young doctor, opposite end of the spectrum from the guys
playing cards, and she lived a few doors away from whatever the hell I just
left.

Life is strange.

Soon, my car was running, and cool air blew from the vents. The strong Ohio sun had made the interior uncomfortable.

My face went to my hands, and my shoulders began to bounce up and down. I lost my composure after my experience at the poker game. Like I said, Janelle and I did not discuss her time away, the dark period of her life. I thought I had a general idea of where she was, what she was doing, who she was hanging out with, but the afternoon showed me I did not.

Oddly, that wasn't why I was crying. I missed Daniel. The boy I did not love like my own was tearing my heart into pieces. I stayed strong in front of Janelle, kept a false front for the FBI, but as I sat in my car, alone with my thoughts, I wondered where he was, who he was with, and who stole him from us.

I thought I might find a clue at the first address on Janelle's list, but I was no closer to finding Daniel than I was two hours before.

Without another voice to bring me back, I went to the bad places in my head, the thoughts that screamed child abuser, rapist, and pedophile. What if we were wrong about Rondo? What if Daniel was stolen by some pervert? What if some desperate want-to-be mother saw Janelle one day and decided to take Daniel for her own? What if some racist scumbag did not like the black child with a white mother and took matters into their own hands? There were countless "bad" scenarios with regard to Daniel's abduction. Up until now, until I had turned the key and waited for the car to cool, I focused on the one or two positive scenarios. With this moment of downtime, my mind wandered toward evil.

No one tapped on my window to ask if I was okay, though several people walked nearby or jogged past the car and stared through the windshield. I cried uncontrollably for a while, sobbing, blowing my nose, calming down, and starting the cycle again. There would be no relief from my feelings until Daniel was found. I couldn't get away from the grief, and just when I was about to regain composure, a new wave hit me.

Finding Daniel

I did not have my phone. It was in Janelle's purse. I was used to checking it for the time. I stopped wearing a watch a few years ago because of the ever-present digital clock in my pocket. The car dash read 5:25 p.m. That explained the joggers outside of my car. Work was over. People were getting home, working out, playing with the kids.

I was in a hot car searching through my wife's checkered past for a clue into the abduction of our child.

My stomach growled. Not only had I eaten just one meal today, but I had thrown it up in a stairwell.

I needed some food before my next trip down Jan's rabbit hole. It's one of the lessons I learned in high school, college, and graduate school, to take care of my body or my mind will begin to falter. I would be in an intense study group session, feverishly quizzing my classmates on material, when all of a sudden I would stop and get some food and drink. I'm not saying this was the same situation, but it was the only useful bit of training I had for my current task. I needed to keep myself fed, hydrated, and alert for the upcoming night.

It took me another five minutes to stop crying, but I found a way to keep my emotions in check long enough to drive toward Oakley, a nearby neighborhood that was next on Janelle's list. I knew Oakley. We often went there as a family to enjoy Dewey's pizza before the restaurant spread across the city.

I did not have time to order pizza. This meal was about speed and substance. Back in the day, when Stewart and I would hit the town on weekend nights, we typically ended our evenings at Skyline Chili in Oakley Square. It was open late and had a great crowd of regular employees. I don't eat that type of food anymore, but I knew it would serve my current purpose, and it was close to my next location.

I went inside the restaurant, used the bathroom, washed my hands, and made my way to a booth. Most people I know call the Skyline cheese chili hot dogs "jammers." That's what you do, jam them in your mouth. I ordered two with a large Coke. The food was ready almost immediately, and I devoured my meal in a few seconds. I must have looked like a man in trouble, lost, hurt, broken, because I caught a few employees and patrons giving me worried glances.

Just like the people who saw me sobbing in my car, no one tried to console me.

Without my cell phone or another person to talk to, my mind drifted.

I thought about couples therapy, and how so much of what happened there, what Janelle spoke about, what I thought I understood but really didn't, all came into focus. Not just the "be honest" part, other stories and statements. One of my stumbling blocks was trying to pinpoint the "why." Why did all of that happen? Why was Janelle a drunk, a gambler, a homeless vagrant?

We talked about Janelle losing her job, losing her self-worth, losing her identity as a management consultant, and all of that seemed rational and easy.

Reflecting on Phil's poker game, I slowly gained more understanding. The game had excitement, high risk, and potential for big reward. Voids created by Janelle's unemployment.

I always thought that was too simplistic, that Janelle had not fallen because she lost her job. Now I knew it was true, Janelle gambled to replace the high-risk, high-reward life she lost when she was fired. Management consulting, similar to many other high-profile jobs like investment banking, hedge fund management, even trial attorneys, can be that adrenaline rush of high-stakes gambling. She would stalk a client, stay up late at night for weeks preparing a pitch, and she would always be in competition with other highly qualified firms. It was as if they were standing around a large pot, trying to land the big prize.

Phil, to a certain extent, was a powerful person, CEO or president of his enterprise. Janelle pitched to those people when she had a job, and maybe sitting at a card table with Phil brought some of that feeling back, that sense of importance.

When she was laid off, she had no outlet for her competitive drive, until she found Phil's game.

With Daniel's fate still up in the air, and my next trip into the sketchier side of Cincinnati about to happen, I still felt a sense of calm as I solved parts of Janelle's puzzle, pieces of her disintegration that had long baffled me. Understanding that she did not leave because of me, because she was unhappy with "us," or the kids, or our life—well, that was something positive.

Then again, as the therapist had advised, maybe none of this was relevant.

I wanted to talk to one of the people at the restaurant, maybe scoot into someone else's booth, slide in across from a fellow Skyline Chili customer and spill my new feelings, get their perspective, but that was crazy. No one was making eye contact with me. I had been crying, and my eyes were puffy. Tears left streaks on my face. I may have been dressed nicely, but my disheveled appearance made me the skunk of the establishment, avoided at all cost.

It didn't matter. I didn't have time to talk. I finished my drink, went back to the bathroom to freshen up as best I could, and left. I thought about those weekends fifteen years ago, walking in with Stewart, getting a big hello from the cook and waitresses every Saturday night. It's amazing how quickly time moves, and how lives change.

Phil's card game terrified me, more so than I'm even letting on, if that's possible. I was so far out of my element, so far out of my comfort zone, I almost shook with fear when I relived the few minutes I was there. I'm sure Phil had a gun, or a bat in the closet, or the fat guy on the chair, Joe, had a gun, and they could probably hurt me or kill me without fear of repercussion or penalty. I wasn't carrying a phone, and no one in that room would testify against Phil. I could disappear and no one would ever find me.

Why did Janelle send me on this trip? It would have been so much easier for her to talk to Phil. Hell, he might have recognized her, said hello, given her a hug instead of the death stare I received.

What was this next place going to be like? If Phil's was the top game, how scary was this Oakley address? Whatever was in store, Janelle could have navigated it more quickly and with more ability than me.

Why was any of this happening? Who took Daniel? Why was he taken? What the hell was going on?

I drove ten blocks from the restaurant in search of the next destination on my list, and found myself on a typical tree-lined street in Cincinnati. Instead of an apartment, I appeared to be looking for a house. I double-checked the street name on the piece of paper, and scanned the homes as I rolled by. Nothing jumped out at me as "gambling hall."

I parked up the street from the address and made my way back, walking on the sidewalk. A mother came toward me pushing a stroller, and a young girl rode a white and pink bike just behind her. There were people mowing their yards, and joggers made their way around the area.

This was a normal street on a normal day in a normal neighborhood.

I stopped in front of the house number on the list I held in my hand. I checked the address a third time. This was the house. Something that had not caught my eye earlier: There was an alley that ran behind the homes. Most of the garages were detached, opening into that back alley.

Finding Daniel

There were no driveways coming out onto the street where I stood. It's not uncommon for neighborhoods to have an alley street. In a neighborhood that relied so heavily on street parking, it made complete sense to have a back alley for utility trucks and trash pickup. Removing driveways allowed for larger front yards too.

It was also easier to run an illegal gambling establishment if the customers used a back entrance.

I went up the front walk to concrete steps and a small landing porch at the door. I couldn't see anyone inside. I didn't see any furniture either, just faded hardwood floors.

I heard mumbling, a low rumble of voices, not loud enough to bother a neighbor or to be heard from the sidewalk, but on the porch, I could make out a crowd of people, a gathering of something generating noise.

The smell of cigarette smoke was thick in the air. The house reeked of it, like the basement was a giant ashtray of used butts and ash taps.

I knocked, rang the doorbell, and waited. After what seemed like five minutes, a skinny guy with a buzz cut poked his head around a wall. He looked nervous. His eyes were too big for his face, accentuated by his sunken cheeks. Everything smelled like cigarettes right now, but even from ten feet away, I could tell this guy would somehow, even though it did not seem possible, make the smell of cigarettes stronger. If I had to guess, he probably smoked more than he ate. He could have been a drug addict, but his big eyes were not glassy. He was not jittery. He was just super-skinny from what I assumed was nicotine addiction, which I guess, in a sense, did make him a drug addict.

I did not wave or nod my head. I stood there in my polo shirt and linen pants. My left arm gently throbbed, and I tried not to move it. Moving it made the pain increase. I should put some ice on it when I have time. That's what people like me do; they don't continue with their evening with a throbbing, painful arm.

He gave a quick glance behind me, saw I was alone, and walked to the door. I expected him to yell through the glass, or maybe open the main door and speak through the storm door, but neither happened. He opened the door, pushed the storm door, and spoke politely and plainly.

"May I help you?"

I was taken aback, unprepared for his normal tone and demeanor.

"Um, hello, I...," I stuttered, confused for a moment by his courtesy. Television dictated he would ask me if I was a cop or speak sternly through the glass. Opening the door? Being polite? What the hell was that?

I was right; even though the open door intensified the aroma of cigarettes, this man made it worse. His fingernails and teeth were tinted yellow, and his skin was a dull gray. I pondered the eternal question, can you smell a fart in an outhouse? I had always thought you could not, but he made me rethink my opinion.

"Hello, my name is Gabe Addison. My wife, Jan, used to come here. Brunette woman, thirties?"

"Jan? Yeah, come on in. You want in on a game? You need some action on something else?" He stepped aside. I could tell he was saying whatever I wanted to hear to get me inside. He did not know my wife. "We don't use the front door out of respect to the neighbors. It cuts down on questions if we use the back, so next time, use the alley."

Seriously? Being considerate to the neighbors?

"And I don't know where you parked, but we like to go a few blocks away, you know, for the people who live around here." He did not offer his name. Maybe Phil and Joe were the only name I would ever get. The top banana had no worries about me knowing his name, but lower-level guys, they liked to stay anonymous. Whatever, I wasn't here to make friends or link in with anyone.

I couldn't keep a smile from creeping across my face. Dani maintained my social media presence. She was basically my publicist. I thought about her receiving LinkedIn and friend requests from the various characters I met throughout the day. "Hey, Gabriel, who is Skinny Cigarette Man? His title is 'attendant.' What does that mean? And here is a friend request from a guy named Phil. No last name, just Phil."

That was the world I knew, links, friends, tweets. That world was normal to me. Was it odd that a person I just met would now want access to my business connections? Maybe a little, but social norms had changed quickly, and connecting with someone electronically was almost expected after a handshake.

This house and world did not appear to use social media or electronic communication.

"I'm not here for a game. I have some questions about my wife. Our young son was kidnapped. I was just over at Mount Adams. Phil said I could ask around to see if anyone here has any ideas about who or why this happened."

As you know, Phil had not given me permission to use his name, and I assumed it was a risk to drop it, but I calculated the odds of a skinny nothing like this guy bothering to call a boss like Phil to check my references. He might bring it up later, "Hey, ran into a friend of yours the other day..."

I decided to take the risk because I knew using the name "Phil" would move my outcome along, and I was running out of time.

Skinny paused for a moment. I could tell he knew Phil, at least knew who Phil was, that it was a big deal that I would have the man's blessing. He was contemplating what to do next—let some guy in who was obviously not there to gamble and might cause problems, or go against Phil's wishes.

"If Phil sent you here, I ain't gonna tell you otherwise, but you can't stop the games or bother anyone. This is a business. There are a few of us running it, and we'll tell you what we know 'cause Phil is asking, but not if you make a scene." He narrowed his eyes. "Make a scene, I kick your ass."

I looked at the skinny guy in front of me. Even my slight frame and average height dominated him in size, but there are some people who win fights because they are scrappy. They will keep punching well past the point they are beaten, or worse, beyond when they were supposed to stop when they have won. It's the General Sherman approach to fighting, total victory. Skinny was telling me, start a fight with him, you better win, or you'll be walking with a limp the rest of your life, if you have a life.

"With that established, come on in."

This man's courteous tone was unrelenting. As I thought about it, let my brain work like it normally does, commenting in my mind about almost everything that happens around me, I realized, he was in the service industry. I did not know how many more places like this there were in Cincinnati. Actually, since I had not made it to the basement, I wasn't quite sure what kind of place this was, but anyway, in the spirit of competition, there might be other places. He was running a business, and doing it in a customer-centric manner.

It made sense. Phil's card game was big money, high stakes, and run by Phil. It was serious and brutal, and for real card players. This was a step down, so while it was also serious, with the potential for high wins, probably more of a potential for high losses. It had to appeal to more people. Phil's game had the allure of big money and playing with the big man. This house had to be at least a little friendly. I'll tell you, the cigarette smoke would have sent me packing, but if that was a given at all the locations, maybe the polite attitude helped keep clients happy.

He continued. "We run a business here, kind of like a bar. We have regulars, people who drift in for a night, people who stay with us for a while then move downstream or maybe even up to Phil's." He paused.

"Who was your wife again?" Skinny was a talker.

"Jan. Forty, brunette, attractive. She liked to drink. She lost money, a lot of our money. She is friends with Randy Rondo."

"Ah," Skinny suddenly realized. "Yeah, Rondo, okay, I remember your wife. We asked her to stop coming. You know that?"

"I didn't even know she was coming here in the first place." Not that I owed Skinny a response.

"I mean, we loved Jan's money. She was a regular goddamn ATM for us, but she drank too much, and she lost too much in bad ways. And, man, what a mouth on that chick." His pleasant smile had given way to a frown.

What did he mean by that comment? Janelle did not use profanity, much, certainly not enough to give her a reputation.

"Isn't that a good thing for you, the losing of money?" I asked.

"Not really, we want people to lose, that's no secret, but someone who comes in, drinks that much, throws money away? It makes our clients think we don't care about them. We run a nice, honest game here. It's not Phil's game, but it's not throwing dice in a back alley neither. Do I care about these people? Not most of them, but they have to think I do. They have to believe we are running a clean game, looking out for everyone's best interest. Jan was out of control. She disrupted the flow."

"What does that mean?" I was really curious to see the basement, this respectable illegal gambling facility.

"We have a blackjack table. Jan would be sitting on a seventeen. Most people aren't going to hit, right? Card counting or not, you don't hit seventeen. Well, she was drunk. She was unhappy. She would hit, bust, done. You'd think that was her business, right? Well, it's not. The guy sitting next to her might be sitting on a nine. He wants the jack that Jan just took. Now he is pissed because she is ruining the game. Now he doesn't come back, and he tells other people we let drunk rookies ruin the games. I can't have that. We can't make a living off of drunk rookies, off of casual gamblers. We need die-hards to fill our roster, and to cultivate die-hards, we have to keep the games serious. Rookies gamble on riverboats. We offer a better product. We sent Jan down."

"Where is down?" I knew it was the next address on my sheet, written in Janelle's perfect handwriting, but I wanted his perspective.

"Any place they are happy to fill her up and take her money. Randy was taking care of her then, using her for cash. I think she was crashing on his couch or something. His chick was pissed, I know that. He got arrested a few months back. Randy shot some guy."

"I know."

Skinny made a statement he believed to be a fact. "You know Jan had Randy's baby?"

"He told me it's not his. That's why I'm here. I need to find out who raped my wife, fathered her baby, and probably stole the boy from my home last night." Wow, that was a mouthful, and it summed up my day. As I thought about the surprises I'd been hit with in the last twelve hours, well, it was staggering. My wife was raped AND our child was stolen.

"You won't find what you are looking for here, but you can certainly try. We might not be as high-stakes as Phil, but we run a pro shop. Like my example of tossing Jan out, we have a clean game with serious people. The last thing we want is some rapist." Skinny shook his head. "Man, if Phil finds out a girl got raped? He's going to lose it. No one wants a rapist, that's bad for business."

Notice it was not bad for women or society. Rapists are bad for business. It was the same sentiment echoed by Phil, that no one likes pedophiles. The brutality of a pure capitalistic situation. I doubted Skinny had true judgment on rape, had never considered it to be good or bad, but if it hurts his revenue? No rape allowed. You want to drink, do drugs, do whatever? Skinny was fine with it, but start playing sloppy and hurt his bottom line like Janelle had? You get thrown out.

With his description of their business model completed, Skinny turned and headed toward the back of the house. I followed. There was a small living room or den toward the back, and there was some furniture, the first I saw in the house. Two tired-looking high-back armchairs flanked a table against one wall, while a faded green couch sat opposite. A Tiffany-style glass lamp adorned the table between the chairs, and the table had lion's paw-designed legs. In my opinion, a rug would have finished the room nicely.

"Do you live here?" I asked him after seeing the room.

I heard some thumping on the ceiling. There were people upstairs.

"Some days it feels like it." Skinny gave me a typical work response. This was his job, how he made a living. It could have been a car wash or convenience store for all he cared. The last thing he wanted was trouble, a disruption to his money stream. An asshole dressed like a golf pro asking patrons if they raped his wife and stole a baby was not good for business. I knew I was getting into the basement because I dropped Phil's name. I guess I could have paid to get into the game. I brought money if that was necessary, but I took the calculated risk of lying to Skinny.

We walked into a kitchen. The appliances were not stainless steel, nor were they old and rusted. The stove was black with a glass top. The matching refrigerator and dishwasher still bore yellow Energy Star savings stickers.

Smoke billowed from the open door leading to what I assumed was the gambling hall. The low rumble I heard when I was outside was now a loud cacophony of voices.

"Is this a bunch of card games like the one at Phil's?" I was curious as to what I was descending toward. I also wanted to reinforce the idea that I had come from Phil's and definitely had the big man's consent.

"We have two tables going. We run a couple of craps games, a sports book, two blackjack tables. It's a basic setup. We also have a number of side options, booze, drugs, and women. This is a full-service place." Skinny pointed toward the ceiling where the thumping was pretty obvious. "I wish I could offer you more hope, but I doubt you're going to find what you're looking for here. You might even recognize a few of our customers. We don't cater to scumbags. Well, we do, but nice scumbags."

Nice scumbags? Oddly, I knew exactly what he was talking about. My best friend, Stewart, might be considered a "nice scumbag."

We went down the steps, and the basement opened into a large gambling hall, similar in look to a riverboat or casino, just smaller. The entire floor was cleared of walls with only metal support beams running throughout the basement. It was built tastefully with a maroon carpeted floor, and a drop ceiling of sound-absorbing tiles. I was well versed in ceiling tiles. Dani and I examined them endlessly as we remodeled or built new offices.

No one looked up to catch a glimpse of me. People stared at their cards or the green felt tables. I scanned the room, recognizing whom I thought to be two fathers of kids in my braces. No one jumped out at me. No one screamed "rapist" or "child-abductor," but honestly, if they had Daniel, they wouldn't be here tonight. I wanted to talk to the owner, see whom Janelle was with two years ago. No one in this crowd was in the immediate suspect pool.

Young women in skimpy dresses or tight jeans and T-shirt outfits strutted around the room delivering drinks. I saw them sell cigarettes and pills to different people as well. This really was a full-service house of debauchery.

Skinny led me toward a table in the middle of the basement. It was a desk with a leather top and a beautiful rolling chair. A man was sitting in the chair, watching us since we stepped into the room. His arms crossed in front of his chest. He looked mean, not in a tough guy kind of way, but in a high school asshole kind of way. You know the type, hangs with the cool kids, makes fun of everyone, and solidifies his position because other people do not want him turning on them. That was the look, smarmy confidence blanketed in asshole.

He stood when I approached the desk. His arms by his side, one holding a cigarette.

"Who the fuck is this?" he asked Skinny, ignoring that I was even there.

"He was just over at Phil's. You remember Jan? Brunette, hot piece of ass, drunk as shit, spit out cash like she was an ATM? We threw her out two years ago? Saddest day of the year when we watched that money go?"

"The loud-mouthed chick Randy knocked up?" the stone-faced guy asked.

"Yeah, well, this is her husband. Someone nabbed his kid. He's asking if we know anyone who might have taken an interest in Jan."

He looked me up and down, the hand not holding a cigarette rubbed his chin. "Jan, yeah, drank too much, talked too goddamned loud, had to kick her out one too many times." I went with a nickname, like the one I gave Skinny. This guy was Smoker.

"She's turned herself around, thanks. She was raped by someone during the time she was coming to places like this. I am wondering if you noticed anything odd when she was here, maybe someone else following her."

Smoker did not look pleased. "Hey, I don't appreciate you sayin' places like this, like I run some sort of shithole full of losers. Phil sending you or not, change your tone or I'll knock you on your ass and throw you in the fuckin' alley. Place was good enough for your big-mouthed, drunk whore wife." He turned to Skinny. "You even check to see if Phil knows this guy?"

This is where I pushed my luck, played the long shot. I was in an illegal gambling hall after all.

"Phil and I spoke less than an hour ago. If you have a problem with me, I will go back to him, interrupt his game, and ask him to come with me. I guess you can call him, interrupt his game yourself, and see how that goes. Joe looked extra pissed tonight. I'm sure he'd love getting off the stool and coming all the way over here." Bluffing was part of poker. My bluff was based on the idea that Smoker was not that close to Phil. Using Joe's name, making it appear I had two friends in Mount Adams, helped my chances of getting out of here with my face intact.

Smoker looked at me, squinted his eyes, and decided against calling me out. "Just show me a little more respect, all right, asshole? I don't appreciate you coming down here, Phil or not, and accusing me of housing rapists."

I breathed out. How my knees were not knocking, shaking with fear, I have no idea. Maybe it was the Coney dogs. I had no other reason to possess such courage. I apologized and moved forward.

"I'm sorry, I mean no disrespect. Jan is my wife, and I lost her while she was drinking. When I say places like these, I mean places she used to go when we were separated." I noticed a wedding ring on Smoker's finger. Maybe I could play off that ring, assume he had an ounce of humanity. Unfortunately, as I later found out, he did not.

"Randall Rondo hung off her, spent her money. He watched out for her, made sure he was the only one with the PIN to that ATM. I mean, a piece of ass comes in here, trashed all the time? I can't tell you the number of times I wanted to take her upstairs. Am I right?" Smoker looked at Skinny and laughed, like it was funny to brag about raping a guy's wife to the actual guy.

"Then Randy got her pregnant."

This was going to be a painful conversation. Phil's name made Smoker talk to me, but it was not going to make him a polite or nice person.

"I just found out this morning that Rondo was not sleeping with Janelle and is not my son's father. He was pimping Janelle out to some bastard, and I'm trying to find out who that bastard is."

"Whoa," Skinny mumbled from beside me.

"He's lucky he's in prison." Smoker nodded. "That son of a bitch was making money whoring out Jan, and he didn't offer her to me? I could have made a mint, classy older woman like that." He smiled at me, nodding, enjoying the pain he shot at me. "Either way, he owed me a cut."

I ignored him, focused on the room. One of the first things I noticed, beyond the thick haze of smoke, was that most of the people in the basement were white. The two black men in the room stuck out.

"My son is black. It seems like you would know the few African-American customers."

"We are an equal opportunity business, but, how did you put it, places like this? Well, places like this tend to self-segregate. There is a black version of our place, a Korean version, a Chinese version, a Hispanic version, and rarely the twain shall meet." Smoker pulled another cigarette from his shirt pocket. I noticed Skinny also had one blazing. The pack was gestured toward me, and I waved it off. I was pretty sure we were getting enough nicotine from breathing the air. Smoker pulled the classic chain-smoking move, lighting the new cigarette from the ember of his old one.

"Why are there so many different places?" This visit was a dead-end. I was asking out of curiosity.

"You know, each place has a few different games. Maybe one has a cockfight, one has a dogfight, one does the tile game. I don't know. I run this one, and we have that Texas hold'em table, which is popular. The sports book is more popular here too. I have white women, skinny, young; that is typically what guys like you look for. The other places will have different offerings, maybe sell more weed."

"You think I have a shot of finding this guy?" I scanned the room again as I spoke. I tried to act confident and comfortable.

"No. You really think the rapist is going to admit to it if you ask him? I might have screwed Jan. I'm not going to tell you." He paused, his grin widened. "Actually, I might tell you." Smoker blew smoke out through his nose. Was that a polite gesture, not blowing it in my face? Was it a trick that smokers do? I've never smoked, so I really had no idea.

One of the girls approached us. She whispered into Smoker's ear. He glanced toward a guy sitting on a couch. The man wore a goofy grin, like he was some sort of stud for bagging a prostitute. Did he think it was his smooth talk? Did he feel like she picked him out from the room? When I was in college or back in my single days, hooking up with an attractive bartender was akin to finding Bigfoot. Getting this young girl to take you upstairs was not finding Bigfoot.

Smoker gave the guy a stare.

"He good for it?" he asked Skinny.

"Yeah, he's fine. He's actually up a hundred in our book, but he's lost a lot more than that in the last two months at the table. He always pays. He's an investment manager or some shit at a small firm downtown."

Smoker reached into his pocket, pulled out a key, and handed it to the girl. She smiled. I hoped she was eighteen. She looked about that age, maybe slightly older with her makeup, but she wasn't buying liquor without an ID or maybe at all.

She went back to the investment manager, grabbed his hand, and the two went up the stairs.

This place was disgusting.

"Hope you don't have your money with that asshole." Smoker laughed before breaking into a brief, raspy coughing fit.

I waited for him to stop before I posed the obvious question. "Where would you go?" I hoped asking his advice and thus stroking his ego might, and it was a pretty big might, get him to help me.

Smoker took a long drag on his cigarette. The red ember glowed brightly, burning until it hit the tan cotton end. There was a pause before the smoke blew out of his mouth and toward my face.

"I'd go to the jail and ask Rondo, but if you can't do that, your next stop is where he used to hang in Walnut Hills. I'd be real careful there. Phil doesn't hold as much juice. His name might get you in the door, but it won't necessarily get you back out." The phlegmy laugh came again. He and Skinny both had a nice chuckle at my expense, at the idea of the husband, dressed like he is going to a golf game, trying to question people from his drunk wife's past.

"You want to hang here for a little while? You know, blow off some steam? We got just about anything you could want." Skinny was ever the salesman.

"I'm good, thank you. My son is still missing. I have to keep moving." I tried to sound sincere in my appreciation, but to reiterate, the place was just plain disgusting, and Smoker was mean.

"You know where we are, cleanest girls in town." Skinny threw me one more line.

I stood there for a few moments, unsure of what to do. Smoker and Skinny puffed away, watching the room, making sure they were making money.

"What did my wife like to play?" I had not asked questions about Janelle; it had not occurred to me until this instant.

Smoker nodded his head toward the blackjack tables. "She would sit there, drink, lose, drink more, lose more. She would show up plastered, Rondo sitting on one of my couches, taking up space I need for customers. Hey—" He looked at Skinny. "You remember that time the guy tried to make out with her, and she pushed him away, and he wouldn't stop? Rondo had to pull this big son of a bitch off, and I threw him out? Jan just kept betting and drinking, like it was no big deal. That guy was a waste anyway, but it was funny as hell watching Randy try to handle him." He turned back to look at me. "And that time we bet her $5 she wouldn't make out with Sheena?" His voice was angry, full of rage at the idea that he had to speak to me because of Phil, that answering my questions was a reminder that Smoker was not the top dog. "And she not only kissed Sheena, but all the girls that night? She was a messy drunk, and we had fun with her before I kicked her sloppy ass out."

I turned and left. I didn't say anything else. I didn't ask Skinny to walk me out, or where the Walnut Hills game was, which I actually needed to know, as Janelle had put question marks next to the address. I spun on my heels and did a normal walk up the stairs and out the back door.

"Good luck finding the guy who screwed your wife." I heard that raspy, coughing laugh follow me up the stairs, mocking me as I shut the back door.

I wanted a shower and a change of clothes, not only because I looked ridiculous in my outfit at these places, but also because I smelled like an ashtray. I felt dirty, inside and out.

Smoker was an asshole, asserting whatever superiority he could over me. I did not care. He did not get my goat or make my blood pressure rise.

Did I want to stand there and let him tell me stories about Janelle? No, but I didn't care what he said. Jan was not Janelle. I'd separated the two, much like my wife did two years ago. I'd use the comparison of shedding her skin like a snake, but that would make my current wife a snake. The caterpillar into butterfly analogy also seemed too simple. I almost had to combine the two: Jan the snake shed her skin and became a butterfly.

You may not believe me, that I didn't care what Smoker said. The truth is, that night was about Daniel, finding him, rescuing him. I didn't care about some punk running an illegal prostitution ring out of a house in Oakley. He was a loser. I was using him for information. He may have thought differently, but I achieved my goal from my visit. The guy who raped Janelle was not a regular at their club. That club was tight, well run, secret, private, a money-making machine. Skinny knew everyone and everything about the people who walked down those steps. He knew their jobs, their debts, their winnings. He knew where they lived, what their family situation was. I could tell that Skinny was the brains behind that house, and in due time, he would be running it. Helping me and believing he was currying favor with Phil was a great career move for Skinny. If there was anything to know, Skinny would have told me.

Walnut Hills was my next stop, my next attempt at finding my son's kidnapper. It appeared to be an African-American gambling hall, which either improved my odds or worsened my odds, I wasn't sure which.

I stood at my car door and reached into my pocket to click the unlock button on my key fob. I didn't hear Smoker come up behind me. I'm not trained to listen for sounds like that. It was still daylight, bright out when he sneaked up, if you can even call walking up behind me sneaking. There were a few joggers down the block, plenty of noises to distract me from hearing him.

I felt a tap on my shoulder and turned to see who it was. Smoker caught me in the eye with his fist. His wedding ring made a tiny cut next to my eye. My knees buckled, and I started to go down, but he caught me and pumped to punches into my stomach.

"Joe says hello. If either of us ever sees you again, we're going to kill you. If it was dark out right now, I probably would. You're lucky I respect the neighbors."

He let me slump to the ground on all fours before he kicked me in my face. "Not the teeth" was all I could think as I covered my face before the next blow.

"Tell Jan she's welcome back anytime," he told me before his final kick. "We love whores her age."

I heard his laugh followed by a raspy cough as I managed to open my car, crawl into the driver's seat, and shut the door. I lay on my side in the hot car fighting off nausea.

The sun was down. I rolled my car to a stop in front of the next address on the paper. I touched the ink, caressing the paper slightly. The handwriting was my only link to Janelle, and I yearned to touch her, talk to her, just hear her voice.

The cut next to my eye was swollen and nasty. The bleeding had stopped, basically because it swelled almost immediately. My eye throbbed, and just a light touch from my hand made me say "ouch."

My nose was not broken, but it was messed up, growing in size like I'd been hit in the face with a fastball pitch.

I didn't throw up, which is amazing considering the two chili hot dogs I had in my stomach.

This was actually my second stop after taking my beating. I made it to a gas station to use the bathroom and clean myself up. The wave of pain I felt when I stood was intense. I doubled over for a few seconds, maybe a few minutes, and took my time to straighten. I walked slowly into the UDF, a chain of convenience marts and filling stations in the area. I wiped my eye in the bathroom, but as I've said, it really didn't bleed all that much.

I looked at myself in the mirror. "What the hell are you doing?" I asked the image.

There was no reply. I did not know what I was doing. I had gone two places, been physically accosted in escalating fashion at each, and yet I was not on my way home. I was cleaning up to go further down the line.

I exited the bathroom, bought a water and a popsicle, and left. I put the popsicle on my eye as I drove to the question marked address on my sheet.

I was lonely. This quest was tough on me physically, but more so mentally. I was used to having a partner. I have never really been alone. I have Dani at work, Janelle at home, Stewart at the club. I had a tight group of friends in high school, a close-knit pack in college. I do my own work, but I am a man of companionship, constant companionship.

Tonight I was on this search alone.

I had only been alone one other time in my life, when Janelle left me. My parents stayed for a few weeks. Her parents stayed, awkwardly, for a few weeks after that. Friends dropped off dinners at first, but after a few months, it was me and the kids.

I hated it. Hated it more than any other time in my life, and tonight brought all those feelings back.

I'd done my pity party, cried in the car, looked pathetic at Skyline. If I learned one thing about myself during this day and evening, it was that I'm actually a fairly strong person. I did not realize I had so much internal strength.

Have you ever wondered if you were tough enough to handle yourself? If you would run into a burning building? Stand up to a bully in a bar? I was doing all of that for Daniel tonight, and while it was painful, it gave me a surge of confidence to move forward.

I had not thrown a punch, but I'd certainly taken a few today, and I was still going. I wasn't at home, hoping the FBI could find my son. I was in my car, sitting in front of a gambling hall in Walnut Hills, mustering the courage to walk inside and maybe take another beating.

When Janelle went away two years ago, I buckled down. I handled the twins by myself. I went to sleep with them some nights, all of us in my big bed, each of us missing the woman in our lives. They clung to me for security and stability, and I was their rock, the parent who promised he would never leave like their mother had. It was a different kind of strength, paternal, necessary. It was far from walking into a gambling/whorehouse and standing toe to toe with a thug. If I needed it, the strength was there. I was one tough son of a bitch. The question was,

was I tough enough for a Walnut Hills, wrong-side-of-the-tracks gambling hall?

The evening air was cool. I grabbed my cashmere sweater from the backseat of my car. Now I really looked like a men's catalogue photo: linen pants, cashmere sweater, polo shirt, and leather fashion sneakers.

I went to the address written on the paper first, and opened the door to get out of the car. I stood gingerly. My abs were tender as I went to my full height, and I was pretty sure I had a cracked or bruised rib. I walked toward the house. I thought about the Oakley place and decided to approach this house from behind. I did not hear noise. It was a family home. There were playthings, a plastic castle, a backyard with a fence.

An older woman's voice caught me by surprise. "You're at the wrong house." She said bitterly. "If you are looking for the whorehouse, you need to go to 3751. You're at 3571. You're probably so high you don't know where the place is."

I turned to look at her, and she shook her head at the sight of my face. She showed no alarm at the growing lump above my eye and slow trickle of blood from my swelling nose, just pity and anger.

"Thank you," I replied politely. My voice was getting nasally as my nose lost function. I didn't say anything else. She would not have believed me, whatever I was saying. To her, I was some gambling drug addict, invading her neighborhood.

I drove over to the correct house. There were no children's toys in this backyard, and there wasn't a privacy fence. I parked in the front. I didn't care about etiquette to the neighborhood. My stomach hurt when I walked. I didn't owe these people a two-block trek to and from my car.

There was a small wooden staircase, just five steps, with a landing that led to the back door. A bank of windows showed a sun porch. A door leading into the house was shut on the far side of the room. I pressed the doorbell, and the inner door opened immediately. I assume they saw me coming and waited for me to make the move to enter the home.

I smelled cigarette smoke and weed. It reminded me of the outdoor festival concerts I attended during the '90s. The volume from the basement was high, loud enough for me to notice from the outside. I assumed this house could get away with more noise than the house in Oakley.

A very large man—I cannot emphasize his enormousness enough—I mean, really big in height and weight. Imagine the largest person you've ever met, and make that man an inch taller and one hundred pounds heavier. He made Joe from Phil's look tiny. Anyway, this big guy came through the door. He had to turn sideways to make it through, ducking under the doorway as well.

"What?" was all he asked. His voice was deep, loud, and intimidating.

"Randall Rondo used to bring my wife here?" God, I hoped Smoker had not called.

"You the guy who Randy knocked up his wife?" the huge man replied. I hesitated, debating whether or not to correct him, but in the end, I just agreed.

"Yes." Yep, that's me, the guy who Randy knocked up his wife. I thought back to social media and contemplated changing my title to reflect my new moniker.

"What do you want?"

"I was in Oakley. They kicked me out." I pointed to my face. "You got a call, didn't you?"

"Yeah," he said loudly. I doubted he had a lower voice, though I also thought about the noise impact on his hearing. Workplace hearing loss is a serious issue, and his loud voice made me think he was a victim.

He held the door open for me.

"Thanks." I nodded to him and made my way around the behemoth.

"Check in with Gerard when you get to the bottom. He said you'd be coming. He can get you chips, women, whatever. He's the dude in the argyle sweater." With that explanation, the big guy went back to his stool by the door. He was not reading *The Economist*. He sat silently, staring out the back. It was kind of creepy.

As in the previous place, the noise of the basement was louder when I made it into the actual structure. The smell of marijuana and cigarettes was also stronger. I coughed for a second before walking down the stairs.

Smoker was correct; this was a mirror of the Oakley place, just filled with African-Americans instead of Caucasians. There was only one card game, a few more dice games, and the women were a little fuller in build. Thankfully the women were more age appropriate too.

I spotted a man in a dark-blue argyle sweater. He stood at the far end of the room, and his eyes had not left me since I entered. It was not hard to pick me out; there were only three other white guys in the room. The three I saw were dressed in button-front silk shirts, hipster outfits if you forced me to categorize. One of them had a woman seated on his lap. His eyes fixed on her with steely concentration. Someone must have forgotten to tell him that she was available at a price, and his quick wit and gaga eyes were not required.

Gerard—I was so excited to have a first name—nodded toward me. I walked through the maze of games, couches, and hostesses until I was standing in front of him. I'm not sure how long it took me, but I'd guess a few minutes. I had my right arm bent to protect my stomach and ribs, but I was bumped a number of times and had to stop to deal with the pain. My teeth gritted, and once I had to use the back of a couch to stabilize myself. Anyway, I made it to the boss.

"Move next to me." He directed. "I like to keep my eyes on the room."

I complied.

"Randy is the guy who knocked up your wife," he said immediately and without looking in my direction. His eyes stayed fixed on the room, moving back and forth like a predator's.

"I know that is the general belief, but I spoke to him this morning. He admitted that he is not. He let some guy rape my wife, took money to do it. I'm here to ask if you remember anyone who paid Jan closer attention than others."

Gerard broke his gaze from the room and looked at me. "John messed you up."

Smoker's name was John, how boring.

Gerard did not smoke like Smoker/John. He did have a glass of cola, which he sipped from occasionally. I doubt there was alcohol in the glass. This man was a professional.

"John's an asshole. He sent me a text, said to be on the lookout for you. Whatever, you're just looking for your kid, right?"

I nodded. Coming down the stairs had strained my newly injured abdominal muscles. I wasn't sure I could talk at the moment.

"He sent your drunk-ass wife down here." He paused for effect and looked at me again. "Does this look like a step down from Oakley? What, 'cause we have black customers we want some drunk woman ruinin' our games? I put Jan on the couch, made sure she could lose as much money as possible betting on ponies and basketball. John is so damn stupid, doesn't understand economics." He took another sip. "I heard about how John would have your wife make out with his girls, mess with her when she was really drunk. Jan was fine. Randy kept her under control. Did she take up a spot, maybe get too sloppy every now and then? Yeah, but, man, did she have cash at first. You a dentist, right?"

I nodded again. My right forearm and hand were still holding my stomach.

"Damn, I should have been a dentist. Good, honest money, and buckets of it. My mother always told me to be a doctor. Well, choices, right?"

Another head nod from me.

As fascinating as Gerard's life choices were, I wanted to get back on track. "So you don't remember anyone?" I got out gruffly.

"Anyone what?" Gerard kept his eyes on the room. I was suddenly feeling like we were a vaudeville act, going back and forth.

"Who might have paid Rondo to rape my wife," I clarified. I spoke clearly, realizing it did not hurt as much as I thought it would to speak.

Gerard shook his head. "Let me explain it better for you. I'm a businessman. I run a franchise for Phil and some of the other guys in town. I do a good job here, I move up. I do an average job? I probably keep doing this until I get run over by someone. John is an idiot, and Stan is going to be running that franchise within the next few months."

"I'm not following," I admitted, partly because I didn't care about his business, I just wanted him to answer my question.

"If I know who knocked up your wife, I am going to tell Phil. After your little meeting with John and Stan—Stan is the skinny, nervous guy actually running the Oakley place—anyway, after that, Phil got word out that he wanted to know who this rapist is. If any of us know, he wants the name. Phil is going to kill that guy or beat the living shit out of him, do the same to Rondo if he can get to him in jail. I know who the rapist is, I tell Phil, and I win. Phil likes me more. It's in my best interest to know who screwed your wife and to benefit from that knowledge."

I was a little concerned at the numbness I'd built up toward the expression "guy who screwed your wife."

"Why would Phil care about any of this?" I asked, genuinely confused.

"It's bad for business, letting people pimp out drunk customers, rape women. Phil can't let that happen. Frontier justice and shit."

I actually understood. "So you don't have any idea? No new faces came through the door those months?"

Gerard stated it one more time, simply and slowly so I understood. "I thought it was Randy, just like everyone else. If I had a clue, I'd tell you right now."

"Damn it," I said aloud, frustrated at the situation.

"Yeah, dude, you're screwed. You can keep swimming downstream, visiting the places your wife hung, but in the end, know that if any of us had better information, we'd be knocking down Phil's door to tell him."

The girl who had been sitting on the white guy's lap approached us and interrupted our conversation.

"You gonna run away with him?" Gerard smiled as he handed her a key.

"As far as he knows," she replied, smiling equally wide.

"That's my girl," he told her.

Gerard waited for the girl to leave our earshot. "That idiot John, he has Stan walking the floor, learning his customers, running shit while John just stands around smoking and looking like an asshole. You met Terence upstairs, that big mother fucker? He's my Stan. He stays at the door, not down here learnin' my shit. I know my people. I control the room. John won't even know what hit him. Stan's good. He's a tiny dude, but he's smart. He'll run a better house than John, get some big ass idiot like Terence to work the door. Big and stupid, that's how I like 'em."

He looked at me. "We done?"

"Yes." We were. I was chasing my tail. "You gonna rough me up?" I asked.

"Not unless you want me too. I could have Terence beat you down."

"No." I nodded with respect. "I'm going home."

I walked out. It was the fastest fifteen minutes of my evening, and probably the most honest and helpful. I looked at the clock on my car's dash, 11:15. It felt like 3 a.m. I'm guessing, because I haven't seen 3 a.m. in a while. It had been a long, long time since I stayed up this many hours in a row. If you're a parent, you're probably thinking, "how can that be? You have an eighteen-month-old in your house." Well, I didn't get up much with Daniel, and by much, I mean, at all. I would wake up, roll over, and go back to sleep. I changed diapers during the day, but Janelle did all of the hard work. She was basically a single mother once the sun went down.

What was wrong with me? Why was I such a horrible parent and husband?

I was physically and mentally done. I was up early because of Daniel's abduction. We were bombarded with stimuli from the police and FBI. I'd been threatened, beaten, scared, and lonely for the last five or six hours.

The question in front of me was, should I go home or to the FBI?

I drove home because I wanted my bed, maybe my wife, but definitely my bed.

It was only a ten-minute ride. As I've told you, Walnut Hills borders my neighborhood of Hyde Park. I spent the time thinking about the evening, about what I learned about my wife.

She was still living at home when she was thrown out of Phil's card game. She was drinking, probably a full-blown alcoholic by then, but if she had cash at the Oakley place, well, she was still using our money. She seemed to still have cash at the Walnut Hills place too, so either she was still with me then, or she stashed some cash before I threw her out.

I thought about her fragile ego, having been fired from her job, her identity, and then, for all intents and purposes, being fired from Phil's. That must have really pushed her over the top or the edge. Which was it? The top or the edge? I guess the edge. God, I was tired. I could not get my idioms straight. Anyway, she is fired from her gambling life, moved down to Oakley, then is fired again.

That's when I threw her out. At least, I assume that's when it happened. I basically fired her from our marriage, from being a mother. I could see how she began to spiral out of control, picking up speed with each successive failure.

Look, I'm not taking responsibility for what happened to Janelle. As you learn in therapy, if you take it seriously, which I never did because I am an asshole. Anyway, you learn that Janelle's problems are hers to accept. Those are her burdens, and I will help her recover, but I cannot place her alcoholism on myself.

Regardless of the therapist's suggestions, I had always wondered about the "why." What pushed J to her life of depravity? What made my wife turn into a drunken, gambling whore? I know now that she was never a whore, but that's what I always called her in my head. I'd look at her from across the table, and she could read it in her eyes, that I was wondering, "why did you leave me to become a drunk whore?"

Janelle told me earlier in the day that she was worried that I would stop loving her when I found out where she went two years ago, but the opposite was happening. I was gaining insight in her life, and because of that knowledge I was healing.

Ten minutes, that's all it took to get from Gerard's to my house. Janelle was ten minutes away that whole time. I was so lost in thought I almost drove past my home.

The two black American-made sedans parked in front of my house snapped me back into the moment. Overnight street parking was frowned upon in my neighborhood, but I guess this fell under the extraordinary circumstances situation.

My bed was suddenly very far away.

For a second I thought maybe, just maybe, the FBI or police had succeeded, they were inside with Daniel, and Janelle was crying, holding our baby, that my life was going to return to normal, and the shower I was going to take would wash away the day, the kidnapping, Janelle's past, everything.

I did not have my phone, could not have been notified. Perhaps everything was over, and I could begin to be the husband and father Janelle and Daniel deserved.

I pulled into my driveway, opened the garage door, parked the car, shut the door, and saw an intimidating figure standing in the doorway to my kitchen. Jerry the tall FBI agent wore a frown. It appeared as though I had disappointed him.

Any thoughts I had of Daniel being home safe faded.

"Dr. Addison, where have you been? Why did you leave our offices?"

I moved from the shadows of my driveway into the light of my side door. My broken face was illuminated. I'm sure if I had not been wearing my sweater, large purple bruises would be visible on my left arm.

"What the hell have you gotten yourself into?" was all Jerry could say, shaking his head as he moved to let me inside.

"Did you ask my wife?" Maybe Janelle had given them an excuse; she was better at lying. I didn't want anything I said to conflict with her.

I could smell the cigarette stench all over my clothes. There was no denying I had been somewhere, and saying a bar was an obvious lie, because you weren't allowed to smoke in bars anymore. Even standing outside with someone else who smoked would not account for how horrible I smelled. My hopes rested in Janelle already providing a plausible excuse.

"She said you fought and stormed out, but no one at my office heard or saw anything." Jerry was pissed, I could tell. Despite his professional demeanor and obvious crisis management training, this guy could not hide his pissed-off-ness. The last thing he wanted to deal with was an out-of-control, beaten-up father.

"Then why are you asking me?" I stood in front of him, trying my best to look upset and jilted. My right arm was holding my stomach, while my left arm dangled uselessly. I thought the pain might subside, but the dull throbbing that was all over my body was getting worse, like it was in an echo chamber, intensifying with each surge of blood.

Janelle stood in the doorway between our kitchen and living room. Had they been standing in doorways waiting for me all night? She had a look of sadness and concern. She walked toward me for a hug, touching my eye, and causing me to wince and pull back. Tears came to her eyes. I could tell she blamed herself for my condition.

We embraced, but she pulled away almost immediately.

"Oh, my god, Gabe, where the hell have you been? You smell like an ashtray." She knew exactly where I had been, but her acting was remarkable. "Go shower and maybe throw those clothes away. We might have to cut off your hair to get the smell off of you. Of all the days, you had to run off when I needed you the most? And what's with the eye and nose? Were you trying to defend my valor again, or were you just in the mood to get your ass kicked?"

"I just…"

"You just what? Felt like taking care of Gabe? Decided to take on the world one asshole at a time? Really? Our son is missing. What kind of a man are you?" She was laying it on a little thick.

"Okay, let's calm down." Jerry moved in between us. "Dr. Addison, why don't you shower and change?"

"Not before I find out what has been happening. Do we have any idea where Daniel is? Do we have any leads? Has anyone been doing anything since I left?" I went with indignation again, it seemed to work this morning. The entire situation was bizarre. Janelle and I didn't fight, not really ever. The therapist said it was part of our problem, that we internalized our marital issues, did not face conflict.

I wanted to know if they had leads, if maybe I didn't have to go back to the seedy underworld of high-end/middle-class gambling.

"You mean since you walked out and went to a smoking, drinking, and fighting party? You have the gall to ask me, to ask the FBI if we've been doing anything, when you've obviously been off on your own doing God knows what? You have some nerve, Gabriel Addison."

She used my whole name, well played.

I spun on my heels and headed toward our bedroom. There was nothing to learn, no leads. Janelle was telling me that with her anger. I'd call it mock anger, but it was true anger. It wasn't directed at me; well, it was directed at me, but it wasn't toward me. She was mad at the world right now.

"Are you running away like you did this morning? Coward!" Janelle yelled as I left. She burst into tears with the word coward.

"Gabe, hold on." I recognized the voice. It was Stewart Givens. What was he doing here?

"Stew?" I kept walking. "I have to cool off upstairs, get changed, clear my head."

"I'll come with you," he said, falling into step with me.

"What are you doing here?" I was done acting, confused as to why he was in my house. Janelle hated Stewart.

"The FBI started combing through your friends and family for suspects. You know I'm going to be the top of the list. I'm your only friend. I'm black. Daniel is black. There you go." He smiled and laughed. Stewart didn't care if he was inappropriate, as long as he got a laugh.

"Yeah, I guess that makes sense." It didn't. He was my friend, sure, but he was also the last person Janelle would call or allow in the house during a time of crisis.

"When you went all crazy, ditched the FBI, pitched your phone into Janelle's purse, they called me to see if I had any idea where you were. Where were you anyway? You smell like you went to a strip club. Well, I guess not, they don't allow smoking anymore." He stopped. "Not that I know that." He laughed again.

"I was out, just out. This is tough, bringing everything back up again, having to deal with the Rondos. Court is one thing, but this? This is different."

Stewart stayed in my bedroom. The bathroom door was ajar, and he spoke through the crack. I put my clothes into the hamper and jumped into the shower. Sometimes you wonder why you spent the extra money on a tankless water heater, and then you have nights like this one, a night when I wanted to wash the filth off myself for an hour.

My stomach was beginning to turn a shade of maroon, and my upper left arm was purple. I thought there might be finger marks where that big man wrapped around, but it was just one band. Luckily, the stomach pain was worse than the arm pain and appeared to cancel it out. My eye was beginning to swell shut in the corner, affecting my vision ever so slightly. The hot water burned as it hit the fresh cut. My nose was officially closed. I carefully cleaned the dried blood from underneath, not touching the swollen nose itself, as it caused searing pain.

"So that's all you're gonna tell me? You were out? You look like a bar fighter, smell like a chimney, and you think I don't know you were checking out all of Janelle's old places? I went there with you, remember? I drove the streets with you, to bars that don't care about the smoking laws. Rondo's in jail, Gabe. He's not out on the streets. You know that."

I wanted Stewart to leave. I appreciated him being there to help, I really did, but this was a family matter, specifically between me and Janelle. We were handling it. We were going to do what we needed to do, and all Stewart Givens was going to do was get in the way.

"I had to try," I said loudly over the shower. "You know I appreciate you hanging out, making sure Janelle is okay, but I'm back, and tonight might get ugly. You should go home and get some rest."

"Shot a 78 today, best round in a long time," he bragged, changing subjects to talk about golf. I found it very inappropriate and a sign that he wasn't leaving. Who in their right mind would bring up a golf score? Who would admit that he played golf knowing his best friend's child was missing? Janelle was right. Stewart was a complete asshole, but he was my friend, and it appeared he was sticking around to help.

The shower felt incredible. After three soaps and hair washings, I turned off the water and stepped out. "You're not leaving, are you?"

"That's not what friends do. Maybe I can try to pick up where you left off tonight, follow the trail if you tell me where to go. I don't think the FBI is going to let you out of their sight. They were pretty pissed. Not half as pissed as Janelle, but still."

"Do we have any idea where Daniel is? Do the feds have a clue?" I was in my closet picking out comfortable clothes for the night. I touched my flannel sleep pants, debating whether or not to put them on. I opted for jeans and a T-shirt.

"No. I got here at like 7. They were panicked and pissed about you leaving, and grilled me about your spots. I laughed, which didn't go over too well with your hot wife." Why did he always say that? "Because you don't have any spots. You won't even stay around for a beer at the golf course, scurrying home or back to the office as soon as we putt out on eighteen."

"Shit," I muttered to myself before speaking to Stewart. "Where the hell is he? I got nowhere. Nobody had any idea who would take Daniel. They all fingered Rondo and told me he was in jail."

"He is in jail, but people like that? He could get this done, steal that baby for his mother. He's a crook, Gabe, a lowlife who doesn't give two craps about other people. He's the guy. You know he is."

I came into my bedroom to find Stewart sitting on my bed. I don't like other people sitting on my bed. I know, it's crazy, but where has he been all day? Where else has Stewart been sitting, and now that stuff is on my bed? This isn't a hotel.

"I don't know if it is him, Stew. He's a dirtbag, sure, but he is such a small-time punk. Who is going to steal a baby for him? You're telling me Randall Rondo has a good enough friend to come into Hyde Park and steal a baby? That's life in prison."

"I do think so, Gabe. It's the only thing that makes sense. I'm sure he has a cousin or buddy who would do it. What about that girlfriend? Who cares where you live? If they think Daniel is theirs, well, they are going to take him. Plain and simple, case closed."

It made sense if you still believed Rondo was Daniel's biological father, but he wasn't. I was the only one in the house who knew that. Still, it was the most logical scenario. Maybe Randall lied to Jerry the prison guard this morning, despite Jerry saying that was impossible. Maybe Rondo is smarter than we think, and sent us on a wild goose chase to give him time to smuggle Daniel out. When the facts were presented, Rondo masterminding Daniel's kidnapping made the most sense. Everything pointed back to Rondo. Nothing else added up.

I took a seat next to Stewart. I lowered my voice, practically whispering in his ear.

"So I have a family, you know, from the practice. Father is a prison guard. He paid a visit to Randall this morning, and get this." I paused for effect. "Rondo says he's not Daniel's father, that two years ago some random guy approached him, paid him serious cash to rape Janelle. When Janelle got pregnant, ran back to me, I think Rondo took credit to please his mother. The whole thing got out of control with custody battles and visitations. Randall couldn't back out of it because of his mom, or maybe he didn't want to back out of it. I don't know. He told the prison guard that Daniel is not his kid, and he has no reason to kidnap him."

"Gabe, are you seriously believing that crap? That some mystery guy was paying Rondo to treat your wife like a sex doll? Doesn't that story seem a little too neat and tidy? It exonerates Rondo and sends you off looking for someone else, while the whole time you should be focusing on the Rondo family. You're smarter than that."

He was right. I was a fool. I should have come clean with Janelle. She would have set me straight from the beginning.

I put my hand on Stewart's shoulder. "Hey, thanks, you're right. I've been an idiot today. Look, it's going to hit the fan downstairs. I have to deal with the FBI being pissed, Janelle being pissed. You should get the hell out of Dodge while you can." I cracked a half smile. "Thanks, Stew, you're a great friend."

"The best and only friend you got." He smiled. "You're going to find Daniel. You will, just drill down on Rondo. Don't believe his lies. He's the one who's taken your son. Let the FBI handle this. This is what they do. They don't straighten teeth, and we don't find missing children. I spoke to them. They know it's Rondo. That's the one and only lead you need to focus on."

We stood together. I sensed it was a moment for a friend hug, but I did not take it. I don't know why, just something I never did with Stewart. Also, my stomach hurt, my arm hurt, and I was worried I might bump my eye or nose on his head.

I am actually a very affectionate person. Janelle brought that out in me. I was shy with women, an introvert almost. I was comfortable with my friends, but not in large social settings. She stuck with me through the awkward phase of our relationship, when she probably couldn't figure out why I wasn't being more forward with her. Now I hold her hand, kiss and hug her as much as I can. I shower our kids with affection too, except Daniel, of course. I treated him like I just did Stewart. Instead of a hug and kiss on the head, I was prone to give him a little fist pump or high five. That might be acceptable if he were my nephew, or even if he were our only child and Janelle didn't know better, but she had seen me with the twins, seen how much love I showed them.

God, I am an asshole. That one second, that fleeting moment of not hugging Stewart, and my horrible, bordering on evil treatment of Daniel flooded my mind. Why had I shut him out? Why had I not realized what I had?

Tears welled in my eyes, my shoulders began to bob, and I brought my hands to my face. It was a bad cry, a wail of sorrow and agony. Everything came out, the kidnapping, the thought of Janelle taking $5 to make out with women for the amusement of the gambling hall, her sleeping on Rondo's floor, being passed around from one shady gambling hall to the next, without a care about where she was going as long as the new place had booze.

And where the hell was our son?

Stewart watched me cry. I think he might have patted my back or shoulder, but he was uncomfortable. The messy side of life, the part that required work and empathy, was not where Stewart liked to live.

The bedroom door opened, and Janelle walked over to me. She pulled my hands away from my face. She had a comforting smile. Love beamed from her eyes. I know that line seems fake or contrived, like some horrible nerd anniversary card, but I literally felt love pouring from her beautiful face into my soul. She didn't speak, she nodded. Her arms wrapped around me, the palm of her right hand went to the back of my head, and she pulled my hysterically crying face into her shoulder.

I didn't care how much it hurt my nose, which it did, a lot.

I don't know how long we stood together, how long it took me to empty my sorrow into Janelle's bosom, but when I recovered enough to open my eyes, Stewart was gone.

"Are you ready to keep going?" my wonderful wife asked me. "Can you still do this?"

"Together, but not alone anymore, it's too hard by myself. We stick together." I was in desperate need of a tissue, actually, a wet washcloth. My entire face was a sticky mess of snot, blood, and tears. "You might want to change your shirt." I waved my hand up and down, pointing out the mess I'd made of her front.

"Had I known you were going to break down like that, I would have grabbed an old burp cloth." That was our marriage, making a joke during the absolute worst time. It was that moment in a movie or television show where it seems darkest, the partners are stuck in a room with the enemies shooting from every direction, yet the one goofball says something like, "you know, I've never liked sugar in my coffee." And it was some running joke from the beginning, and it makes them smile, despite their impending doom.

Janelle and I were at that rock bottom. If we had not found Daniel by now, well, weren't there statistics that said our chances were dropping? Weren't there awful stats that tell us he is dead or gone forever? Neither one of us said anything, but we knew the situation. An entire day had passed, and nothing had come from it. I didn't find anything. Rondo wasn't talking. There weren't any other possible suspects.

Bluntly stated, things were bad.

True impotence was something I'd never felt before, and it was excruciating. I added it to my list of new experiences that I hoped to never have again. I could do nothing to assist the FBI with our case. I had tried to solve the mystery on my own and failed.

I sat in my living room, Janelle held my hand, and I took my verbal lashing from the agents like an adult.

"Where were you for nine hours during the investigation into your son's kidnapping?"

"How can we trust you, if you won't trust us?"

"Am I adding you to our suspect list? Do you really want us wasting time chasing you instead of finding Daniel?"

It lasted for about ten or fifteen minutes. Janelle's rock-solid defense and my constant crying took the teeth out of their bite. Jerry relented and simply asked me what the hell I was thinking and where the hell I was.

"He was doing what I asked him to do," Janelle finally confessed. "I told him to look into my past, the time I was a drunk. I thought he would have better luck than the police. If you want to be mad at someone, be mad at me, not Gabe."

Jerry looked at his partner, then at me. "Did you learn anything?"

"Nothing. I went three places, and they all told me the same thing. Rondo is the father, he's in jail, go talk to Rondo. Then they hit me."

It was late, after midnight, I think. I did not have the car dash to keep me up to date, and Janelle and I don't have clocks in our living room. Whatever time it was, I was exhausted, and I probably looked it.

"Okay," Jerry replied. "What you did was stupid, but we are where we are. Everything points to Randall Rondo. Mrs. Addison, you have a relationship with him, good or bad, it's something. Let's take you to the jail tomorrow morning and see if we can get somewhere. I've spoken to him. He won't say anything to me. Maybe he'll talk to you."

And just like that, without lying or conniving, Janelle and I were going to get the sit-down with Randall Rondo we both wanted and needed.

Just like in the movies, the darkest hour suddenly had a glimmer of light.

Janelle and I lay in bed. I stared at the ceiling, physically bruised and exhausted, but mentally wired.

It was 2 a.m.

"You awake?" I whispered.

"How can I sleep?" I heard her shuffle on her side, and the dim moonlight creeping in from our windows showed her leaning on her elbow, facing me.

"I did learn something today, something I don't want to tell you." I looked up at the ceiling. It didn't matter that it was dark, I didn't want to look at Janelle when I told her about the rape.

"What is it? Gabe, you can't keep anything from me."

"Jerry the prison guard spoke to Rondo."

"You told me, nothing came from it, just like when the FBI questioned him."

"No, he told me something, or Rondo told Jerry, and Jerry told me."

She turned on her side lamp.

I continued to look at the ceiling.

"What?" she asked, not so much in a questioning tone, more like a flat demand.

I did not respond.

"Gabe." She touched my cheek, turning my face toward her. "I can't run from that time. It was horrible and disgusting. I'm sorry you had to see what I was then, a lousy drunk. I did things, didn't care about the consequences. The one thing I didn't do was cheat on you, at least not consensually."

"Rondo isn't Daniel's father."

114

We maintained eye contact.

"A second man paid Randall to rape you. Rondo took the money, I guess it was a lot, and when you got pregnant, Rondo just said the baby was his. If you remember, he didn't accept responsibility right away. We thought it was him, but he denied it until Daniel was born. Once Randy's mother came into the picture, that's when he stepped forward."

She did not drop her gaze, nor did she say anything.

Janelle whispered aloud, as if she were thinking it and saying it at the same time. "You and I have to talk to Randy alone, without the FBI. I don't know how, but it needs to happen. No lawyers, no police, no FBI. You, me, Randy, and maybe your new friend, the prison guard."

I did not reply.

"Goddamn it, Gabe, we could have done that this afternoon. Why would you keep this from me? We could have Daniel back already. If we find out who this asshole is, we find my baby. What were you thinking?"

"I—," I stammered.

"Stop. I'm sorry, this is my fault. Everything, all of it. I can be mad at you, or I can accept the fact that I did this, put the pebble in the snow at the top of the hill a long time ago. I'm the drunken mess that got raped for money. I received Daniel for my sins, but the sins are still sins, and it appears I need to atone."

Was that what she thought? That she was deserving of whatever came our way right now? That Daniel was a reward, but she must continually pay for him with fire?

"I know I don't say this, or talk about my feelings, or share." I gave a weak smile. "But I don't agree with your worldview." I looked at her, my beautiful wife with combed hair that looked maintained even while we were in bed trying to sleep. "Sometimes bad people do bad things. It's not some great big karma situation. You were a drunk, but you didn't deserve what happened to you, and you don't deserve what is happening right now. We did get a blessing in Daniel, but that doesn't mean you owe a tab for him. Walking through life thinking there is some bigger meaning to actions and occurrences, I guess that's fine, but it's not who I am, or who I thought you were."

She moved her hand and touched my face again, avoiding my nose.

"I don't know how I deserve you." She caressed my cheek. "You think you are the lucky one, that I am this smart, attractive woman who you got lucky to marry, and that's all true." She paused. "You don't understand that I am the fortunate person. You are smarter than you believe, handsomer than you understand, and more caring and wonderful than anyone I have ever met. I do believe in karma. You are my example, the way you treat others with respect and honesty, and the success your life has seen. I lost sight of what I had, of how incredible you and my family are. I thought I was defined by my job, but Daniel let me find focus. I'm a wife and mother and partner and friend. All the other stuff is just filling time. That's not to say that a career is meaningless, but for me to focus on it was."

She paused for a moment.

Her hand rested on my cheek. "You've been so angry for so long. I made you bitter, mean at times. I'm so sorry I did this to you, to us, the twins, our family. I hope you can let go and be the old Gabe, the one who doesn't think of mean things to say in his head."

How did she know me so well?

"You always had funny thoughts, but now they are mean and twisted. You think I am sad because you don't love Daniel, but I'm sad because I made you into what you are, and I have to face it every single day. I see you upset with yourself, what you've become."

She stroked my cheek.

"I love you, Gabriel. I know you forgive me for my breakdown. What I hope you learn to do is forgive yourself for taking me back."

"We're going to find him," I told her. I didn't know what else to say. Tears fell down my face. Two years of therapy, two years of being together after her fall, and this was the first time she'd ever said something like this to me, and just like my wife, she knew the inside of my head the whole time. Even when I didn't know why I was so mad, she did.

"I know we'll find him. Even when I don't think we will, I still believe we will." She stopped stroking my cheek, resting her hand on it instead. Her touch was warm. Any other time I would have closed my eyes and enjoyed the feeling, but tonight my son was missing.

"We're not getting any sleep tonight, are we?" It was a rhetorical question. I don't even remember who asked it.

If people are keeping score, I was back to killing Randall J. Rondo. I was going to have to wait until he told us everything we wanted to know, but then? That son of a bitch was going to pay for what he did to my wife and family.

Finding Daniel

Jerry the FBI guy asked us to arrive at the field office by 8:30 a.m.

I checked in with Dani at 7 a.m. I knew she was on her way into the office, that's how she rolls, early to work to get the day moving. She yelled at me for even thinking about the practice, refusing to speak with me about anything other than Daniel, Janelle, and me. She told me she was praying for me, and to not call again until we had Daniel back in our arms.

I hung up the phone, sitting on the edge of my bed just like I had twenty-four hours earlier. Janelle was in the shower.

I may have slept an hour, but I wasn't sure. If I did sleep, it wasn't registering. I couldn't tell what was a dream and what was me staring at the ceiling with thoughts of worst-case scenarios in my head. I'm sure my mind turned off for a few moments to reset. It had to, right? At some point my body must have given in to the mental and physical punishment of the previous day.

The phone did not ring all night. That was good news. Sure, it meant they had not found Daniel alive, but it also meant they hadn't found his body. That was the image that clouded my mind. I pushed it aside as best I could, but my fear was that we were on the wrong track again, that Daniel was kidnapped by a bad person, unrelated to Rondo, Janelle, or Janelle's mystery rapist. That a molester or psycho took our baby, and that Daniel was dead. I was so tired I couldn't fight the bad thoughts. It was a battle in my brain between positive and negative energy, and I was just too weak to keep positive.

I needed coffee.

I did not have the opportunity to make the coffee the night before. I was busy being grilled by the FBI and having a complete breakdown with my wife.

I don't have a fancy coffeemaker. I've tried them. I love coffee, and I'm quite wealthy, but they don't do it for me. I have a $30 maker with a glass pot, and I use pre-ground, grocery store-bought coffee.

I stood at the counter, staring at the machine as it hissed, steam coming from the top and sides. I hated waiting for coffee; it's why I set the timer the night before. I can't stand the few minutes it takes for my machine to crank out a pot. It's not even that long, I know, but today it was endless. Idle time gave my mind an opportunity to consider Daniel's plight.

Janelle stepped into the kitchen. She moved next to me and joined my vigil at the coffeepot. I'm sure we were both frowning, our thoughts wandering toward evil. I don't know for sure, as I didn't take my eyes off the pot, watching the coffee level rise, two cups, six cups, the endless amount of time it took to make it to eight cups. When finished, the machine celebrated its accomplishment with three annoying beeps.

"We're going to find out one way or the other," Janelle said calmly. I turned to look at her after I filled my mug. She looked like hell. There were dark circles under her eyes, her skin was pale, but her hair was perfect, flawless as usual.

"From Rondo?" I asked stupidly.

"If we don't get info from Randy, it means Daniel was taken by someone else, and he's dead." She took a sip. "Be prepared for the worst, but expect the best today." My left hand was resting on the counter, and she reached out and put her right hand on top of it. "Today is the day, no excuses, no regrets. We are a team, and we'll come through the other side."

She sounded like a coach in the locker room before a championship game, and maybe she was. Maybe in her mind, this was it, the big game of our senior year. We can go out on top, at the pinnacle of our sporting life, or we can lose and forever regret our one big chance.

Janelle was in robot mode, void of emotions. I'm sure she switched them off for the morning.

"I love you," I told her. My voice was monotone. Maybe I was in robot mode too, or perhaps I needed more sleep. I definitely needed more coffee. My emotions were gone. I was cried out. I had no more anger to vent. People talk about feeling hollow, and maybe that's how I felt, but not really. There were emotions inside of me, I could feel them, but they didn't come to the surface anymore. It's hard to describe. I wasn't suppressing; it's like I was too tired to bring anything to the forefront of my brain.

"I love you too." Janelle squeezed my hand. "Now, I've decided we need to make Randy request the no cops, no lawyers meeting with us. You need to contact your prison guard friend, get that information to Randy. I'm sure the FBI is working with Rondo, offering him a deal or help on his case. Have him agree to the meeting, but only on the terms of no cops, FBI, or lawyers."

"I can try. Jerry the prison guard isn't my new best friend or anything."

"Jerry is the FBI guy, honey." Janelle reminded me, like I was confused. As I've said, I'm horrible with names. Both Dani and Janelle are constantly helping me with the names of people I'm not around often.

"I know, the guard's name is Jerry too."

"Really?" she replied. "That's kind of funny, and convenient. You know how bad you are with names." A partial smile passed her lips.

"I appreciate any help I receive from the universe with regard to names."

I made the call to Jerry the guard. His phone did not ring. It went straight to voicemail. I stated our request and hung up. I nodded toward Janelle to let her know it was done.

Time was creeping. It was only 7:40 a.m.

I poured cereal into a bowl, covered it with milk, and joined my wife at our circular kitchen table. The chair between us had a plastic booster seat strapped to it. I noticed an old piece of cereal still sitting in the booster. It's impossible to keep things clean with a toddler in the house. Without a dog, food appears just about everywhere Daniel has been. The couch cushions house old cereal, squares of cheese, and fruit chews. I won't even discuss the car and all the interesting things I find between the seats, but let's just say that apple slices do not age well.

Little moments like this, sitting at our family table where we eat meals together at least once a day, whether it is breakfast or dinner, helped me cope. I know, you probably think seeing the cereal piece would send me into a negative mood, make me sad, desperate, but it didn't. I remembered Daniel and how he liked to throw food at his brothers, maybe catch them off guard. He was a smart kid and waited for his moments, but he was just a little boy, and half of the time he dropped the cereal during his throwing windup.

I needed to be a better father. I yelled at Daniel for throwing food last week. I took his bowl away. Janelle didn't say a word. She frowned and stayed quiet. One of my sons told me to calm down, it was all in fun. Jesus, what the hell was wrong with me? Why was I so angry? But now I knew, I was mad at myself for doing the right thing, for taking my wife back.

I finished my cereal, rinsed my bowl, and placed it into the dishwasher. We needed to run it. I grabbed Janelle's bowl too, going through the same procedure. I enjoyed the routine, getting a detergent tab, pressing the button. I almost felt normal loading the glasses and coffee cups left by the FBI the day before.

"When this is all over, when we have him back, you can make it up to him, Gabe." Janelle could read my mind. I've told you that already. "He loves you. I know you think you've been horrible to him, and we can debate that, but he doesn't care. He loves you. He lights up when you come home. He runs to sit next to you at this table. As much as you've tried to push him away, he loves you because you are his father."

I stood at the sink, hands on both sides, head down, and I listened to her console me.

Goddamn, I've been an asshole, but if I get the chance, if we get him back, if the sweet Lord smiles on us for one second today, I promise I will never be that asshole again.

Janelle and I were getting ready to leave for the short drive downtown when a car pulled into a driveway. Behind the black sedan were two patrol cars. Did I mention the one that was parked in front of our house when we woke up? A police cruiser that I believe was circling our neighborhood all evening was now parked in front of our home to either watch out for problems or make sure Janelle and I did not make a break for it.

FBI Jerry knocked on our door. His tall frame filled the entryway, and his head appeared to extend above the top.

"Good morning," Jerry's deep voice said to me after I'd opened the door to let him inside. "We have a small change in our plans. Michelle and I thought we'd take a few moments to review all of the facts surrounding the case, walk through the events, see if we have missed anything." He stood in the doorway. I guess he was waiting for an invitation.

"Please, come in, that sounds like a great idea." I motioned for him and his red-haired partner, whose name I now knew, Michelle, to come inside.

They made their way through my living room and into the kitchen, exchanging somber pleasantries with Janelle.

"May we sit at the table? It's easier for us to consult our current notes as well as take additional ones." Jerry was all business today, not that he wasn't the day before, but he appeared to have more professionalism and intensity. I did not know why but guessed it was because our odds of finding Daniel were decreasing as the time moved along. I had no basis for that opinion; my mind was filled with doom, and it was an easy leap for me to take.

I pulled out a chair from the table and sat. "Is that our new plan, the small change is to re-create the crime?"

"No," Michelle replied. "We've been contacted by the jail. Randall Rondo would like to meet with you and Janelle. He will not speak with us, the police, or his lawyer, just you two."

Janelle perked up. "That's great, right? It means he might have information for us."

"It is good news. You are scheduled to speak with him at 11." Michelle continued to take the lead as Jerry examined our reactions. "We'd like to walk through all of our information, prepare you for the conversation. I think we are going to get one shot at Mr. Rondo."

I nodded with enthusiasm. Nothing they said would prepare me more than I already was for the meeting, but I'd play along as if they were helping. We still needed the FBI. If Rondo gave up the rapist, Jerry and Michelle would be the ones to get him, not me.

"Why do you think he isn't trying to make a deal with us, lowering his murder charge in exchange for information? Why is he abandoning his lawyer? He's never done that before." Jerry's eyes did not narrow, but his tone was accusatory and full of distrust.

"I don't know," Janelle responded innocently. "I haven't spoken to Randy in months."

Jerry pulled out a chair next to me. It was Daniel's booster seat. "I'm sorry," he said sincerely, pushing the chair back under the table. He let out a sigh. Seeing Daniel's chair made him remember this was a kidnapping case, and we were the wronged party. I could see his body language alter. He pulled out another chair and sat.

"It's been a long twenty-four hours, I know. We should start from when you put Daniel down two days ago."

And we did. For the next two hours we went through everything, again.

When, exactly, did you put him down? Who mows your yard? Did you know this employee had serious credit card debt? Who has your alarm codes? Who valeted your car during your last evening out?

It was then that the questions took a decided "turn."

"Let's talk more about last night," Jerry said, turning to me for the first time, speaking directly to my side of the table rather than politely turning back and forth between Janelle and me.

"Okay," I replied innocently. It was hard for me to forget the previous evening. The Aleve were doing a poor job at dulling the throbbing in my face, ribs, stomach, and left arm.

"I'm going to put our cards on the table, Dr. Addison." Jerry always wore his serious face, but in a way I find difficult to describe, he actually got more serious. I know that sounds impossible, but his determination appeared to increase.

"You have come off as a husband who wanted his wife back two years ago, but did not care for the baggage she brought with her. We have a kidnapping with no apparent motive. The entire Rondo family has alibis, and while you also have an alibi, we are having a hard time getting around the fact that someone got into your home, used your security codes, and managed to get out without detection."

I nodded like a dope. My bashed-in face must have looked like a stooge or something, a patsy just agreeing with the FBI's interpretation of the last day. I honestly did not connect their dots because it was such a leap for me to conclude that I was a suspect. I knew I didn't take Daniel, so why would they think I did?

"Gabe had nothing to do with this," Janelle quickly interjected. She understood what was happening.

"Mrs. Addison, I understand it is difficult for you to look at this objectively, but the pieces are beginning to fall into place." Jerry had turned away from me and was addressing Janelle. "Your husband, we think, went to meet with the kidnapper or kidnappers, and they demanded more money."

Jerry turned back to me. "Is that why you took $5,000 out of your checking account yesterday? You ditched your phone, made up a fight with your wife, and tried to call the entire thing off, but it's too late, and they want more money?"

I've said from the beginning, it was in my best interest for the FBI to find the son of a bitch who did this to us. I never truly believed they would eventually assume the son of a bitch is me.

"That's enough," Janelle said calmly. "Gabe took that money out of the bank because he was buying into my old card game." She got up from the table and walked to our kitchen desk station. We keep a family computer in the kitchen for recipes, to check email in the mornings, and to try to keep our older sons in the same room with us when they need to use a computer. I'd placed the remaining money from the day before in the desk for safe keeping. Janelle opened a drawer and held up the unspent $2,800. She walked back over and threw it on the table.

The time-stamped withdrawal slip was tucked into the packet with the money.

"Here is the damn money. He had to give half away to Phil Towerson. You are in Cincinnati law enforcement, so you are probably aware of that name."

Jerry nodded as he wrote notes on his pad, his face looking down at the table.

"My husband went to a few of my old places. He did not meet with kidnappers. He did not arrange for any of this to happen."

"Can anyone vouch for you being at that game last night?" Jerry asked me, keeping a straight face to what was obviously a ridiculous question.

"Other than the UDF I went to after my face and gut were kicked in, I doubt anyone will say I was anywhere last night." God, I wish over-the-counter pain medication worked more effectively. My head was pounding again.

Jerry looked at his partner. She was not taking notes, and instead had been watching us, meaning me and Janelle, with the eyes of a prosecutor. She must be some kind of truth determining seer, because she gave Jerry a nod. That was the third nod of the table, my idiot nod, and now two FBI acknowledgment nods.

"I think he's telling the truth," she admitted.

"Okay," Jerry said. "Moving along."

That was that. We moved along to the next theory, which was our only theory, that Rondo had taken or facilitated the taking of Daniel. It was not the theory that Janelle and I believed, but to get a sit-down with Randall, we stuck with it.

We finished the marathon session at our table, created a list of questions the FBI wanted answered by Rondo, and headed toward the jail.

I drove my own car, tailing the FBI sedan.

My hands began to sweat.

Want to know something funny? I'd not spoken to Randall J. Rondo once in the last two years. Janelle had always dealt with him directly. I knew his parents, brothers, and sisters, but I'd never spoken to him face to face, or even on the phone. The man was the father of my son, and I had not said two words to him.

I didn't want to speak with Rondo when I thought he'd slept with my wife, and now that I knew he pimped out Janelle without her knowing? That he'd given her to a rapist?

There were a few scenarios that ran through my head. First and foremost was my leaping over a table to attack him. I weighed the idea, whether my new best friend Jerry the guard would help me beat Rondo senseless, or more importantly, protect me if the fight went against me, which it surely would in my current, broken state. My other option was to sit quietly at the table, emasculated and weak.

I don't want to come off as overly testosterone laden, but could I live with myself if I didn't come over the table? Would Janelle still consider me a man, if I sat there,?

"This is about Daniel," my wife began from the passenger's seat. "You probably want to kill Randy, start a fight. You might believe I will think less of you if you don't." Jesus, she was a witch with her mind reading sometimes. "I will think less of you if you can't control yourself, if you can't see the bigger picture of finding our boy. A real man understands this meeting is about Daniel, not Gabe's valor or my honor."

She was right.

"Randy is the only one who can help us, Gabe. He's it. If you don't want to be with me while I talk to him, that's fine. I'm not even sure I want you with me, because you're going to see a side of me that lived on the streets, but if you decide to come in, you sit there and listen. Do you understand?"

I did not respond.

"Gabe, do you promise to let me handle this and not attack Randy? His life is over, he's done, you don't need to do anything to him. He is already in jail, and he did it all to himself. You have me, and a family, and a life. Randy doesn't have a life for you to take. It's already over. Daniel is not his son, we are finished with Randy after today." She put her hand on my leg.

"I'll go in with you, and I promise not to do anything. I don't think I'll even say a word."

I hoped I wasn't lying.

I sat next to Janelle in the prison visitor room. It reminded me of a school cafeteria. There were tables scattered around, small gathering areas for visitors and inmates. A din filled the air. I could not make out specific conversations, rather a mumbling of words mixed together from each grouping. Every once in a while there was a shriek of laughter or despair, a woman crying, or a child giggling.

The furniture was metal. The tables were hexagons. Three benches went around each table, one bench for two sides. All of the furniture was bolted to the floor. The tops of both the tables and benches were metal grating like a picnic table. I did not see people eating, so I'm not sure why the tops were like this. Maybe the guards wanted to be able to see through the table tops, or maybe this furniture was just on sale when Ohio furnished the prison visiting room.

The tables and chairs appeared to be clean, shiny with a new coat of paint. I don't know why I noticed such a detail, but the black metal furniture glistened against a contrasting disgusting floor. The tiles were beyond cleaning. I smelled the bleach they used to disinfect the grimy floor, but the color, the filthy grays and browns had become part of the '70s-style tiles. Nothing they used or did would make them appear clean. I assumed the budget made the prison management choose which to update, the floor or the furniture? I think they chose wisely. No one sits on the floor.

Janelle held my hand. I wasn't sure if she was still mad at me for keeping the secret, for wasting a day, for any of the things I'd been screwing up for the last twenty-four hours, but regardless, her fingers intertwined with mine as we sat on a new or newly painted metal bench in a prison visiting room waiting for Randall.

I doubt she was mad at me, maybe annoyed that I wasted the time, but she was viewing all of this through the lens of someone whose chickens were coming home to roost. In Janelle's mind, all of this was her reckoning, the bill she owed for her time away, for falling apart. Daniel was the reward, and now the tab was due, so anything I did, well, that wasn't really my fault. How could I be blamed for the situation?

Rondo appeared through the glass separating our room from the prison population. He was handcuffed or shackled or however they referred to people in metal chains bound at the hands and feet. I suddenly noticed, or at least acknowledged, large metal rings bolted to the floor in the middle of each bench. Some prisoners must have been latched into those rings during the visits.

Rondo looked young, scared, and weak. When I'd seen him in court, he was a tough guy, and even though it was obvious he was lifting weights—his arms bulged against the orange jumpsuit—he appeared timid. I think it was his eyes. He was terrified. His glance darted from side to side until he saw Janelle. Their eyes met and locked onto each other.

It was not a look of love. Rondo's face wore shame. Janelle's was stone.

A regular looking man held Randall's arm. I guessed it was Jerry, my new best friend. I'd expected Jerry to be some sort of hulk, but he was of average height and maybe a bit overweight. His authority must have come from the system rather than his size. The guard leaned toward Rondo and whispered into his ear. Rondo nodded.

A buzzer sounded over the hum of conversations, and a door clicked open. Rondo and Jerry walked through, and the guard steered both of them toward our table.

I stood and extended my hand to Jerry.

"Here you go, Doc. Enjoy your talk. No thanks needed, you've taken good care of my kids, and my wife likes your office. Consider this a," he paused, "professional courtesy." A smile crept across his face.

"I appreciate the courtesy, Jerry." We shook hands.

Janelle and Randall did not break eye contact.

"Do you know how sad I was when I thought you raped me?" Janelle began before I could even sit down. I quickly realized I was not going to be part of the conversation.

"Jan," Randall replied apologetically.

"Don't Jan me. We were friends. I was devastated when I found out I was pregnant. Not because of the baby, but because it meant you were using me. I was getting used by everyone back then, but you seemed to be different. Yes, you took my money, but I didn't care about money."

He did not respond.

"Who was it? Who did you pimp me out to? Who was I your whore for?"

I winced as she spoke the words.

Randall did not drop his gaze. With Jerry out of earshot, his fear dissipated.

"You bastard. You let some asshole screw me bareback? You let some disease-riddled prick get me pregnant? I was going to speak at your hearing, ask for leniency, play the Daniel card, that you are a good person and deserve to see your son. Fuck you. Fuck you, Randy, and fuck your whole family."

I was suddenly introduced to Jan, the foul-mouthed woman described to me the day before.

"The dude was clean. I didn't know he was going to knock you up. He was kind of old. I didn't think old guys could even have kids. Damn, Jan, I'm sorry. I know that don't mean nothing, but you know how it is. Money, that much money, for him to get off on you for a few minutes? You didn't care. It made Bethany feel better, knowing I was pimping you out."

"Bethany? Your girlfriend talked you into this? That's how you rationalize what you did?" Janelle shook her head. "Who was it?" she asked him again.

"I don't know, some random guy who showed up outside of Oakley one night. I think he was waiting for us."

"You know who the hell he was. Don't lie to me. You know everyone, and you know who this bastard is." She turned to me. "Gabe, tell Jerry he's not cooperating."

Fear shot back into Randall's eyes. "No, no, hold on, Jan. I really don't know, shit, I don't, please. Jan, you don't know what happens in here. You don't know what it means to put me in bad with the guards. Don't even joke about that."

Jerry the guard was right: Randall was out of his depth and terrified because of it.

"Then tell us the name. I'm not joking. You think you're off the hook for lying to me, for pimping me out, for using me for money? You think I can't get to you in here? The hell I can't, Randy. You knew it the second you met me. I'm a tigress, and you don't want to mess with me. My kid is missing, and you're standing in my way. So spill it, you piece of crap, or I swear to God you won't make it another three hours." The Janelle I knew did not swear. It seemed like she was speaking a different language with Randall. She was reverting to her street tone, her street vocabulary, where every other word was emphasis rather than pertinent. Profanity was a necessary element in the conversation.

"I swear, Jan, I don't have a clue. He wore a baseball cap, a Reds cap, and sunglasses, and he drove some big Buick or something. I don't know. He paid me in cash."

"Then you better come up with something pretty goddamn quick." Janelle wasn't using proper English, something upon which she prided herself and insisted on from our children.

"Give me a second." Randall moved his fists to the side of his head, right next to his eyes. He tapped the clenched hands against himself. "Jesus, I'm thinking." His eyes got big. "My phone, the asshole sent me a text, half a dozen, maybe more, and it's on my phone. After the first time, when he showed up, he asked for my number so he could text me."

"You expect me to believe you have a phone from over two years ago? Are you out of your head? That's what you're telling me?" Janelle was right. She was a tigress, and I did not want to be on her bad side.

"My little cousin, Charlotte, I gave her that phone. I got a new one right before I came in here, lied to the lawyers that I lost it. The phone was the top of the line back then, and she still uses it for music. Her mom was telling me the other day about how Charlotte still loves the music player I gave her. You have to get that phone. I bet the texts are still there. You can check the phone number. That's all I have. I don't know nothing else."

An awkward silence filled our table. The noise of the room seemed to fade away. I stared at Randall, keeping a unified front with Janelle. I wish I could say something like, "it took all I had not to jump over the table and tear him limb from limb," but honestly, I just wanted to leave. I was done with the man, the family, anyone associated with that time in Janelle's life. I hated him, sure, but his life was over. He was in jail, on video shooting a man while robbing a store. Randall James Rondo was never going to be a factor in my life again, and I wanted that time to start immediately.

"Here's the deal, Randy." Janelle's voice was confident and firm. "We are going to get that phone and find the asshole you let screw me. We are going to give your cousin a new music device in return for swapping the phone. You are going to arrange that swap immediately. You are also going to tell your mother that you are not the father of my child, and your family is going to disappear from my life, forever."

"Jan," he pleaded with her. "I can't tell my mom, I just can't. It's the one thing I've done in my life that makes her happy."

"You piece of shit. I can't believe we were friends." My wife stood. "Get me that phone. I'll be in Fountain Square at 3:30. Your aunt or mother better goddamn be there, or I swear to God you'll be dead before dinner. Do you understand?" She turned before stopping in her tracks. She leaned over the table and spoke to Randall. "No, you won't be dead, you'll be whatever is worse. I can't even imagine what it's like to be in here, but whatever scenario is the worst? That's where you are going to be, Randy. You're going to be stuck in the worst for a while, until I decide otherwise, or until you're dead."

"Jan, that shit ain't even funny," he pleaded.

"No, it ain't, and it's coming for you, Randy." She straightened. "We're going to the electronics store, and then to Fountain Square. Tick tock, motherfucker."

Did my beautiful, accomplished, intelligent wife just say, "tick tock motherfucker"? I had been in an alternate reality for the last day, but somehow, things actually seemed to get stranger. Before I could nod or motion toward him, Jerry was standing behind Rondo.

"You done, Doc?" he asked me, ignoring the prisoner.

"Randall needs to make a ten-second phone call. Can we do that?" I didn't know if I was pushing it.

"I don't know my aunt's number." Randall was pleading with me, like I was the rational person available, like I would talk some sense into Janelle, make her call off the dogs.

"Then you call your mom, you tell her what to do, and we get this done," I explained. "If Jerry says it's okay." I looked toward the guard.

"The only thing that's not okay is him not helping to the fullest of his abilities. I don't like slackers. Slackers get put in a special place with a special group. I came in an hour early for this meeting, so I'm already in a bit of a mood." Jerry rested his hands on Randall's shoulders, giving them a pat.

"I'll call her." Rondo whispered, his eyes looked toward the ground and his shoulders slumped under the weight of Jerry's hands.

Jerry nodded towards me. "He'll make the call, Doc. Don't you worry."

Randall's eyes were still looking down when he said one last thing to me. "They guy used to send me a text, just one word. That's how you'll know the right number." He told me what to look for on the phone, and I frowned. I thanked Jerry, despite his insistence that his help was simply a professional courtesy, and I left the prison. I did not speak another word to Rondo. I assumed I would never see him again. Once we had his phone, had the name of the scumbag who treated my wife like a sex doll, we didn't need him anymore. Once his family found out Daniel was not his child, their child, well, we never had to see them either.

Who was this mystery man with a Reds cap, sunglasses, and a possibly a Buick? It sounded like he targeted Janelle, sought her out. Could he be some random guy from the gambling halls? Someone who saw easy prey and pounced? If he was, why didn't his name surface over the last day? Why didn't someone know about him scoping out Janelle? She was known in the three places. Sure, they took her money, let her drink, but no one I met did anything else to her. Just like Gerard told me in Walnut Hills, giving up the rapist was probably the best thing for him to do, particularly with regard to Phil.

Janelle was out of the prison. She was through the visitors' door and probably fuming in our car, if she hadn't taken the car to the store without me. When I signed out and the heavy door closed behind me, I let out a sigh. I did not like that place.

Janelle stood with FBI Jerry and his partner. Her head hung low. I couldn't hear what Jerry was asking, but I saw his lips moving. J's hair was pulled back, and I noticed her ponytail sway each time Jerry's lips stopped.

I joined the group, listening to Jerry interrogate while Janelle gave "no" responses.

"He wouldn't talk to me either." She finally lifted her head to stare him in the face. "I don't know what to tell you other than that. He kept saying that he told us everything he knows, he's not involved, his family isn't involved. He even went so far as to accuse us of hiding Daniel on the cusp of the latest custody hearing."

I thought Janelle was going a bit too far, but she seemed to know just how to lie to people, just what they wanted to hear. She was a consultant after all and a damn good one.

"Okay, let's go over the conversation, as short as it was, and see if I can glean anything from it." Jerry was using his serious voice. Did he have any other kind of voice? Probably not.

"What else are you doing?" I asked Jerry. "I get that Rondo is the number one suspect, but he's not talking. What the hell else are you doing to find Daniel?"

"Gabe." Janelle touched my arm.

"No, I'm sorry, Janelle, this can't be their only lead. I understand that Rondo is our best suspect, but there have to be other people Jerry is looking into. Is he still considering me? Is that why he's keeping us with him to go over a conversation we just told him was worthless?"

"It is." Jerry nodded toward me. "You running off, Randall Rondo confirming our suspicions that you might be hiding your son for fear of losing him in court. It starts to add up to your involvement. It also explains why Mrs. Addison corroborates your story from last night. Maybe instead of just you being involved, both of you are involved, and now the kidnappers want more money, beat your face, and you are sending us on a wild goose chase so you can get more money to get Daniel back. I don't think it's a strong lead, but it's a lead, and we're following up on every possibility."

Janelle kept her cool before responding. "You believe it is logical that I would kidnap or hide my son for fear I might lose the tenth and final custody hearing? Seven of the motions were dismissed before trial. Randy is in jail. We are fit. I am the mother. That is quite possibly the dumbest lead I have ever heard."

"Let's calm down." Jerry held his hands in the air. I had not noticed how long his fingers were. I'll never wonder why they sell extra-large gloves again. "Give me an hour. I promise you, there might be something you missed during the conversation you just had. We'll sit down, hash it out. You will be free to go right after lunch."

"Free to go?" I asked, shocked by the expression.

"A poor choice of words, I'm sorry. You will be finished with me in an hour, two hours tops. We have twenty agents following up leads. We have Rondo's old girlfriend at the police station. We have other agents, local and state police speaking with distant Rondo relatives around the entire state. We are going to find your son, but you need to trust us, and most importantly, you need to help us as much as you can."

I looked at Janelle. She nodded to Jerry, shooting a glance at me immediately after. I assumed she was about to come clean, let the FBI know that Randall was not Daniel's biological father. Let them know about the cell phone we were getting at 3:30. I assumed she was going to confess and let the FBI do their job, a job they were much more suited to handle than we were.

Janelle grabbed my hand. "Let's follow him to the station, Gabe. Jerry is correct. That's where we need to be, and telling them about our uncooperative conversation with Randy is what we need to do."

I headed toward the car, my wife's hand in mine. Jerry walked behind us. It appeared that he was going to ride in our backseat. Despite the recent back and forth, I could tell Jerry did not trust us. He did not want to give us the chance to speak and corroborate our story before we went to the station.

It was too late. We didn't need time. With her brief statement, Janelle had set the tone for our story. Randall knew nothing, shared nothing, and acted indignant. If our words were off a little, that might have been expected given the gravity of our situation. If the FBI separated us, we would stick to our stories, getting out of the office with enough time to buy an iTouch and get to Fountain Square by 3:30.

"We can't do secrets anymore," Janelle said matter of factly. We were in our car, alone, five minutes away from the FBI offices after a grueling two hours. They had separated us, hammered us, relentlessly asked us about where I had gone the night before, what Randall had told us, what we were obviously hiding.

I never came close to breaking. I didn't even lose my cool. I remained calm, levelheaded, and acted exhausted, a little frustrated, and above all else, cooperative. My eye kind of hurt, my nose really hurt, and I focused on the throbbing in my stomach, counting the beats of my heart as it sent blood through my wounded areas.

I didn't ask Janelle how she had made it through. She could lie to Saint Peter and still get into heaven.

Jerry spent half of his time in my room, left to, I assume, supervise the questioning of Janelle, and had returned to release me about ten minutes ago. I took my wife's hand again, having released it when we were put in separate rooms, and strolled quickly to our car.

We drove in silence until Janelle broke it.

"I kept the fact that I was raped a secret, you were trying to protect me by keeping the paternity of Daniel a secret, but we have to stop. That's it. No more. We share the good, the bad, and, well, you know."

"I'm sorry," I replied.

"No more apologies. We move forward. Let's get the phone and be done with this. I want my dear, sweet son back. I want my life back." She put her hand on my thigh. "I want our life back."

We drove silently for another minute before I broke.

"Then why are we doing this alone?"

"Alone? I'm here this time," Janelle replied, confused by the question.

"No, not that, why are the two of us doing this alone? Why aren't we using the FBI's resources? Why didn't I tell them about the phone? About the mystery guy? They can solve this much faster than we can."

"Let's get the phone and find out who the person is, then we'll decide what to do." J's voice was flat.

"What do you mean, then we'll decide what to do? What options do we have? Confront the person or people? Forcibly take Daniel back? Look at my face. I've tried that already. It doesn't work. Not to mention the fact that right now, with Rondo exonerated, we are the prime suspects in our own son's kidnapping. We can't go off and take care of this ourselves. We might end up in jail because of it."

"If we get the FBI involved right now, we don't have options," she said.

What was she talking about?

"Just trust me, Gabe. Let's get the phone, and then we will call the FBI."

I gripped the wheel tightly, worried about the options my wife had in her head.

The next thirty minutes were a blur.

I found my way to an electronics store. Janelle bought a beautiful, pink music player with a pair of expensive over-ear, wireless headphones. We met Randall's mother and aunt at Fountain Square, a large open area in front of the Fifth Third Bank building, just a few blocks away from where the Reds and Bengals play in downtown Cincinnati. Rondo made up some story about how the phone might incriminate him, and that the family needed to get rid of it, and we were the most trustworthy. The story made no sense, but served the dual purpose of getting us the old phone, and giving the Rondos incentive to hide the phone's existence from the ever-present FBI and police.

Janelle and I sat in our car with the phone, having made the switch. She scrolled through the undeleted texts. Randall had simply turned off the carrier function and handed the phone to his cousin without concern she might read his old texts or emails.

Within seconds we could see why. The texts were harmless. Some of the texts on my phone were racier—certainly the ones from my old high school and college friends.

"Did he give you a hint as to which number we are looking for?" Janelle asked, hoping Randall had opened up to me after she stormed out of the jailhouse meeting.

None of the texts were attached to a name; messages were listed by phone number. Randall did not have any contacts listed in his phone, not even his mother received "contact" status. She was an anonymous number in a string of texts and received calls.

"He said the texts were one word." I hesitated to repeat the word.

"Well?" my wife said impatiently.

"Bitch. There should be about a half dozen to a dozen texts with the single word bitch." No secrets, as painful as it was.

"Wow, that stings." Janelle said flatly. She was focused as she flipped through the hundreds of phone numbers. "Jesus, how many different people sent him texts?"

"If it helps, I don't think you're a bitch." It might not have been the right time to make a joke, but sometimes I don't understand boundaries or timing.

"If only that were true," Janelle replied as she looked at the phone. "Bingo." Her finger stopped the scrolling numbers when she saw "bitch." A Cincinnati phone number sent the text. I reached across and tapped on the phone to open all of the texts sent from that number.

"Bitch" was written fourteen times, always lowercase, always just that one word, typically sent between 1 a.m. and 4 a.m.

I pulled out my phone and began to dial the number.

"No, don't use our phone." Janelle did not want to spook the kidnapper. It was too late. I have very fast fingers, and I'd typed the entire number into the phone. I quickly stopped the call before the first ring began.

I don't remember phone numbers anymore. I don't think any of us do. I save numbers into my phone after dialing them once, or I save them when I receive a call. When I was young, like ten, I remember knowing all of my friends' phone numbers. You had to call people back then, use your fingers to press the keys. Even when I could not recall the number out of the air, put a touch-tone phone in my hand, and, boom, I could dial my childhood home from rote memory.

It wasn't weird that I did not know the number, did not recognize it when I saw the ten digits on Rondo's phone, did not realize I used the number all the time, called it a few times a week.

The canceled call sat on my smartphone. A name replaced the number I'd dialed, as my phone knew who it was immediately. The phone even had a picture of the person next to the phone number, a goofy picture of a black man with red hair and huge red sideburns, dressed like a Scottish golfer.

Janelle looked at the picture, her mouth opened slightly in amazement. Like me, she had nothing to say, no words to describe the shock and anger. I had a little shock, but more anger, lots of anger.

I might go so far as to call it rage.

"This tells us a few things," Janelle began calmly. I remember these first sentences after we found out Stewart and Teddy Givens were the villains. I know, "villains." It's such a comic book word, but apt for this situation. They were villains, evil people void of good. Anyway, I remember how calm and collected Janelle was. She began to talk so matter of factly. It's almost as if she expected this, that her six months away had been so bizarre, nothing from that time period could shock her.

"For one," she continued. "Daniel is safe." She put her hand on my leg, and I saw her shoulders relax for the first time in two days. The realization that her son was alive and being cared for gave Janelle a respite from the stress. "Teddy is out of town with him. We have to find out where, send the FBI there. Or—" She stopped for a second, wheels turning behind her eyes.

"Or?" I asked her. This is when I got to find out the options she had been calculating earlier.

"I don't know the exact 'or' yet, but I have to look at this as rationally as I can. Stewart paid Randy to rape me. I'm guessing at least fourteen times. I got pregnant. Obviously Teddy knows about the rape and paternity, and she stole my son. If we don't take care of this, those evil people will be in Daniel's life forever."

"You're going dark on me, J." I did not like how her train of thought was moving. It was obvious she wanted something "done" to the Givenses. "They are going to jail for a long time, don't worry. Rape, kidnapping, those are not small offenses. That son of a bitch can straighten teeth in jail for the next ten or twenty years. Hell, maybe the rest of his life."

Janelle ignored me. "Or we could kill them and end this now. I'll fight for Daniel, you know I will. I know you will, but if we take care of this now, tonight, we can end our struggle. The Rondos are gone from our lives. We know that. If we get rid of Stewart and Teddy, Daniel is ours."

I sat silently, wondering how we had come to this point, when Janelle had crossed the line.

"You think I can live with myself if I kill another person? You think I can just hack Teddy Givens into pieces and bury her in the yard? Did you read *Macbeth*? Do you remember "The Tell-Tale Heart"? It would destroy us, eat at us, ruin everything we are." I let my comments sink in. "I'm upset too, furious, insane with rage, but I'm not that insane. We call Jerry the FBI guy, we give him this new information, and we get Daniel back. Stewart and Teddy go bye-bye for a long time."

"If we can find her, she might be in Mexico by now or maybe the Canadian woods," she mumbled. I could tell Janelle was unhappy, in disagreement with my option.

"If she is in Mexico, we can't find her alone. If she's holed up in some cabin in the woods, we need the FBI. I've let you run the show, and it's worked. It brought us here, but now it's out of our hands. If you want Daniel back, this is how we do it."

Janelle looked at me. Her shoulders sank a bit, and she exhaled.

"You're right. It's over. We know who has Daniel, and he's coming home as soon as we find them." Her head began to move up and down slowly, turning into a full-fledged nod. "Make the call."

Jerry reacted as I expected. He did not react. He accepted the information, scolded me for working outside of the lines—mind you, the scold came in a calm and even tone—and asked for Janelle and me to bring Rondo's old cell phone to the field office.

I complied.

J and I were soon sitting in the nice lounge-like room at the Cincinnati office of the Federal Bureau of Investigation, except this visit the FBI had a person standing outside of our door. My wife and I held hands, unified. To be honest, I also held her hand for support. I was nervous, upset, furious, confused, all of the negative emotions wrapped up into one tight little ball, save for the one glimmer of ecstatic joy I felt about cracking the case about Daniel.

Janelle had not spoken since we called Jerry.

"Do you think he hates me that much, or was all of the rage pointed at you?" Her voice was normal, like she was contemplating ordering the special at a restaurant.

"If I had known he hated me, let alone this much..." I mumbled. I had nothing else to say. The guilt was impossible for me to ignore. My friend, a person from my circle, had done this to us. It wasn't Janelle's past, the scumbags from her despair. It was a guy I had in our wedding. A man I called to discuss problems. The friend I asked to help me track down my alcoholic wife during one of her benders.

Was that the night Stewart decided to rape Janelle? Was that the night he decided to exact his revenge for my success? My happiness? My better life? Was that the night, when we found Janelle walking with Randall? He was holding her up, his arm around her for support. It could have been mistaken for romance or love, but it was just a kid extending a helping hand to a tangential person from his youth. It was a man living in the evil places of his heart who took the opportunity to be decent again, to help a vulnerable woman sleep in a warm, dry apartment, safe from the horrors of the street. I knew now it was a low-level thug bilking a wealthy drunk for cash, but at the time, Randall seemed genuine.

I remembered Stewart asking me, "how the hell did he know you? That kid called you Dr. Addison."

"I straightened his teeth. Rondo is his last name. He has four or five siblings. I worked my way through the family." So you found me out. I spoke to Randall Rondo once every four to six weeks for two years while he wore braces I installed to straighten his teeth and correct his overbite, something he acquired from sucking his thumb.

I was buckling Janelle into the backseat of my car that night, not even thinking about my responses. Stewart had stayed in the car, never engaged Randall. He must have thought about the plan right then. Decided to rape my helpless, lost, drunk wife as I tried to hold her up and strap her into the seat. Teddy was babysitting the twins at my house that night. I was oblivious to the twisted world I was living in, too focused on the hell Janelle was going through.

Stewart had sold out to one of the big companies by that night, lost thousands, earned pennies on the dollar of what his practice should have been worth, but those were the times. The world had imploded, orthodontists went under. He was a salaried guy now, not concerned with hooking into multi-kid families anymore. He made what he made, which wasn't as much as he had been making, but much more than his take-home after the world economy crashed. He pretended to be sick as many days a month as possible. If you ask me, he was putting the thermometer against his bedside reading light, if we took temps orally anymore, which we don't, but maybe he was putting the thermometer into his dog's ear. Stewart called me to play golf because he was "hot" at least twice a month.

"How could anyone hate that much? How could anyone be that much of a monster?" Janelle asked. She sat on the sofa, holding my hand, asking questions as if detached from the situation. She was almost clinical in her inquiries. Maybe she was detached. Stewart raped Jan, the part of my wife that existed for a brief time but died when the pregnancy test read positive with Daniel.

"I don't know," I said, staring ahead, looking out the open door into the busy FBI office. "And how could something so wonderful come from so much hate and rage. How could our beautiful boy be created from such anger?"

She squeezed my hand.

Jerry entered the room from the left side of the door. It was a surprise. The wooden venetian blinds were drawn, and we could not see him before he stepped through the door's frame.

"Okay, we have every police officer in Ohio looking for them. We know that Teddy Givens has family in Indiana, Illinois, and Minnesota, and we have agents at or heading toward those people. I can't say I'm not pissed off with your side investigation, but it's broken the case, so what's done is done." He did not sit down. "Do you have any idea where Stewart Givens would run? He was obviously in Cincinnati yesterday. He played golf at your country club; we have him teeing off and posting his score later that day. It appears his handicap is important." Jerry shook his head in amazement. I'm sure he'd seen things like this before, horrible people acting in bizarre ways, but the part of Jerry that was still a normal person was shocked at how a kidnapping rapist could play golf and post his handicap during this entire event.

"According to the pro, Givens shot his low round of the season," Jerry said. "What a cold-blooded snake." Jerry looked back and forth between us, waiting for our insight into Stewart's schedule.

"I don't know," I replied. "I mean, I work all the time. I have kids. I'm at their sporting practice or events. I play golf with him once or twice a month, and that's during the high season. No idea what he's doing with his days. Could you answer where your close friend is right now?" Honesty was my new policy. I did not have a goddamn clue what Stewart

Givens did with his time. Maybe he wasn't working as hard as I was, maybe that's why his practice closed. Hiring Dani pushed me to the upper echelon of orthodontics, but I was still the horse pulling the plow. If I did not have the work ethic I do, did not possess the skills I do, hiring Dani would have been a waste of money. I never call in sick, unless I am sick. I didn't play hooky with Stewart Givens.

"Fair enough," Jerry conceded. "We'll do our job now, and believe me, we're damn good at it. This guy cannot hide for long."

I nodded and smiled. It was the expected social construct. I was supposed to be grateful that Jerry was saving the day. At this point in our journey, I just wanted to go home with my wife and wait for them to bring my son through the front door.

I wanted Teddy and Stewart to pay for their crimes, but more than anything, like Janelle said, I just wanted to go back to our life.

Our saga ended anticlimactically over the next few hours. For all of the twists and turns, the last part of the rollercoaster was a slow and boring straightaway.

Teddy Givens was hiding in plain sight at her aunt's house in Woodbury, Minnesota. It's a suburb just outside of St. Paul.

Daniel was with her, safe, sound, and unaffected by the trauma. He knew Teddy; she and Stewart sat for us often, which is how they knew our alarm codes.

The entire situation unfolded just like the television shows I've watched. I swear there could have been music playing, like in the montage that occurs when the FBI finally knows who the bad guys are, and it ends up being pretty easy to find them, rescue the kidnapped child, and return him to the tearful parents. The scene takes about ten seconds, and the last camera shot is me nodding to Jerry, looking up from my family hug to give him that relieved smile and mouth, "Thank you."

Teddy Givens confessed immediately. She and Stewart conceived the plan together and decided to take "his" child. They felt they needed to steal Daniel from us after watching the custody battles with the Rondos. She told the FBI that we had "too much money" and "too many resources" for them to mount a realistic custody fight.

Oh, and the tiny detail of how Stewart would have to admit he paid Randall Rondo to repeatedly rape my wife? Well, yes, that was also taken into account.

Their master plan was to move to Minneapolis/St. Paul. Teddy would stay with her aunt, and Stewart would transfer to an office in six to eighteen months, depending on when the "heat" had died down. She had been prepping the aunt for her arrival for over a year, telling her she was pregnant, writing about a fake birth, sending pictures of her with Daniel, taken when they babysat. There was one of her in Janelle's hospital room just after Daniel was born. She was holding his swaddled little body, her face next to that unmistakable hospital blanket.

Why are all the blankets in the hospitals the same, white with a teal and reddish striped pattern down the middle? How can every single hospital in the country be buying from the same place? It didn't make sense. Community, private, university, metro, rural, it didn't matter what kind of hospital you gave birth in, everyone had the same unmistakable blanket.

No one in Woodbury had a clue Daniel was stolen.

Jerry relayed the information as we waited for Daniel to return home. He broke from his professional demeanor. I guess now that the case was done he could let his guard down. He actually said, "That woman has lost her mind. They tried to have children for years, and when you got pregnant, regardless of the method, Stewart saw it as his chance to have a family. He is one black-hearted bastard."

"And where is he?" I asked.

"He's our concern now. You take care of your family. Change your alarm codes. The police have an extra patrol coming through your neighborhood until we catch him." Jerry returned to his professional posturing.

"What if he tries again?" I asked.

"Like I said, he's our problem, and we'll take care of him. There's an extra patrol. Change your alarm codes. It's all good. No offense, but the guy's a dentist, I wouldn't get too worked up. He lost his chance, and now his life is over. Stewart Givens, if he has a sane brain cell left in his head, is far away from here."

And that was it.

We met Daniel at the airport two hours later, crying and hugging him as he laughed and smiled. He had no idea what was happening, but he kept saying "Mommy" and "Daddy," with extreme excitement.

It's amazing to me how quickly we fell back into our routine, not the same old routine, not the one where I'm an asshole, angry about caring for my wife's baby, but a routine like we had when the twins were young.

I used to linger at my office, not too late, but maybe an extra half hour, forty-five minutes more than I had to. I don't anymore. I get home, excited, renewed, happy with my new opportunity to have my family.

We told the twins about the ordeal when they came home from camp. "Uncle Stewart" and "Aunt Teddy" were big parts of their lives. I'm embarrassed to say they are, or were, my kids' godparents. The boys were scared for a while. We had some late nights putting them to bed, easing their worries about an intruder or kidnapper, but like many childhood fears, theirs subsided after a few weeks.

Janelle and I talk about those two days. We get philosophical about it, how it brought us closer together, forged the family in fire, that kind of crap. I don't know. It was a nightmare. I know positives came from the experience, but it was so horrible I'm not sure it was worth it in the end. I'd like to think I would have come around eventually, begun to love Daniel without the trauma, realized what I had in my life without losing it for that short time.

I know Stewart and Teddy are evil assholes, but I missed them too. He was a good friend, in my wedding, watched my kids, listened to my problems during golf. We grew up together, worked through marriage together. How did that all devolve?

Janelle continued with therapy. I've gone with her a few times. She asked me to sit in with her, listen to her thoughts, things she talked through, worked through with her doctor. Learning about the rape was not easy to adjust to, but she believed all along that she had been raped. The new wrinkle was the betrayal by a friend, by someone so close to us we left our children with him. How could she trust again? How could she learn to let people into our circle?

I had to learn the same, how to work through my rage. My wife was raped, repeatedly, by a close friend, a guy who called me the day after he'd done it, laughing and joking twelve hours after raping my wife. What kind of sick, messed up person does that? What kind of twisted jerk pats me on the back, cackling after a crass joke in the golf locker room, when he knows he was paying to rape my unconscious, bottomed-out wife?

In one of our last therapy sessions together I asked Janelle the question that was nagging me, stuck in my mind the entire time I wandered through the dark places of Cincinnati. Why did she send me on that journey? Did she think it would make me appreciate Daniel? Would seeing where she spend that time make me understand what Daniel meant to her, and what he should mean to me?

"I sent you because I am a drunk who likes to gamble, Gabe. I could not trust myself to go."

The cigar was just a cigar.

We're still working through everything, but we're working on it together. Janelle and I are a tight couple, no secrets, no lies, and no issues.

Randall James Rondo is eligible for parole in fifteen years.

His mother gave Daniel a big stuffed teddy bear, five feet tall and very fuzzy, and said she would see him around. We don't expect to hear from them. Randall's mother was, indeed, devastated to learn her son received money from Stewart Givens, allowed a man to rape a woman, and lied about paternity for two years.

She cried when she gave Daniel the bear. She hugged Janelle, whispering her apologies before leaving. She looked broken and sad. As any mother would, she had held out hope for a shred of good in her son, hope that maybe the lessons she tried to teach him, the decency she tried to impart, even a tiny bit, had made it into Randall's heart, and now she knew nothing had. He was a bad person. I'm sure she'll carry that sadness with her all the time. Some people, when they are daydreaming, when there is a lull in the conversation, they have good thoughts and a smile might creep across their face. And then there are people like Randall's mother, who will laugh at a church gathering, smile during a story, and then, when the story is over, and thoughts come back into her head, she will frown, her lips will turn down on the edges, and a sadness will fill her eyes, an unhappiness so profound it defines her quiet moments.

I pitied her. I'd been that unhappy. When Janelle was gone, a drunk, I had the same pain, and I didn't wish it on anyone. I pitied this poor woman, who raised five other children to walk the path, who brought joy and goodness into this world through her work and family, but would be defined by her one bad seed. I hoped, and maybe this is a sign of personal growth, that Randall found himself in prison, that the good qualities that brought him to help Janelle off the streets would emerge, and he could put to rest his bad impulses. I sincerely wanted peace for the Rondo family.

I called Jerry the prison guard, thanked him for his help, and actually asked him to watch out for Randall. I did not realize that Rondo was on his way to a far darker place, to a different prison, but Jerry said he would put the word out to the guards there. If Randall James Rondo wanted to be good, if he wanted to change, they would give him a chance. I'll be honest, I'm not that good a person, so I don't know why I wanted to help Rondo, but I did. Janelle smiled when I told her, not because I'd helped her old friend, but because it showed her what kind of person I was becoming. Only a happy person could make that phone call, a person content with his life, and confident to spread that good karma to someone else.

I did not hear from the FBI again. Well, that's not true. They checked in every week for four weeks, then every two weeks, and now they call once a month. I know I'm on Jerry's electronic reminder, because he always calls at 8:15 a.m. on a Tuesday. And you know what? That's fine. I do not need to be on the FBI's speed dial. I hope I never need their help again.

As the months rolled on, the concern people showed me, the worry in their eyes, was finally fading. Dani hugged me for the first month every damn time she saw me. She'd give me that "I love you, I'm here for you," support hug. I needed it, and I appreciated it, and like a true friend, like someone who is tuned into me and my world, she stopped at just the right time.

Other people did not get the memo and continued to ask "How are you doing, Gabe?" or "Is Janelle all right? We were just talking about you." It's fine, I understand. It was a horrible and traumatic thing for our friends and our community. Not only did a child get kidnapped, but the kidnapper was living among us. An evil was walking in our very midst, and no one suspected. What good does locking your doors do, when Stewart and Teddy Givens are out there?

But like I said, the fear was almost gone. The glances of concern and caring were over. I could rake my leaves without stopping to tell people, "We're okay, thank you."

Fall in Cincinnati means football. My twins played on their seventh-grade team. We bought a little sweatshirt for Daniel with the team name on it. He ran along the track around the field, happy, care-free, safe. Janelle takes a lot of pictures, both of the twins and of Daniel, even a few of me. That is her new thing, pictures, keepsakes of each moment.

Despite everything that happened, I am a blessed man.

Dani makes me go to a conference every year, sometimes two conferences a year. You'd think it would be an orthodontics conference, but, no, she has me attend business trade shows.

"What can you sell at an orthodontics show? All you would do is give away our business model, not that I'm worried about that, because, well, they won't have me to implement it, but regardless, I don't see that value of mingling with competitors. You are going to a Midwest, small-to-midsized business show, and you are going to meet and schmooze—oh, and you are presenting too."

"Huh?" I replied. "You want me to do what now?"

I don't argue with Dani. I learned that long ago. And that's why I found myself at the Sheraton Hotel on Water Street in Chicago. It was the week after Thanksgiving, and freezing cold. The hotel is near Lake Michigan, and the wind comes off the water, zipping down the streets and turning them into wind tunnels.

She had done all of the work for me. I had a "deck" of PowerPoint slides to present to a room of business people. The first slide read, "Orthodontics as a Business." It was a spin on the common phrase, "The business of medicine," or whatever service you want to insert at the end. Dani had created a fantastic presentation about looking at orthodontics as a business, like selling coffee, rather than viewing medicine or dentistry through the traditional lens of helping or caring. And, yes, I know orthodontists are viewed about as altruistic as plastic surgeons, but her presentation takes our business model to the next level. Whatever, I was just the mouthpiece, a pitchman to get our name out there with hopes some of the attendees were from Cincinnati.

You see, the largest growth segment of our industry is adults. Kids are there, and we take care of them, but Dani created a boutique option for our adults, away from children, comfortable chairs, no *Highlights* magazines. I haven't mentioned it, because it wasn't appropriate or applicable to finding Daniel, but it's another reason we are killing it as a business. Kids don't mind being treated in a large open room. Given the option, adults prefer privacy.

We started with one boutique three years ago, just after the jobs market turned around a little and people had insurance again; now we have eight. We serve alcohol after 5 p.m., staying open one night a week to accommodate working customers.

So that's why Dani had me at conferences, to beef up our adult client base.

Technically, I never had to leave the hotel. The convention was in the lower level of the Sheraton. There were plenty of dining options onsite, but it's Chicago, right? I had to get out and walk around. Who doesn't want to stroll the Magnificent Mile in a wind chill of twenty degrees?

The hotel is not on the Magnificent Mile, that famous strip of Michigan Avenue in Chicago filled with stores and restaurants. I had to walk a few blocks on quiet streets before entering the hustle and bustle of holiday shopping.

I love Cincinnati. It's my home. It's where I'm raising my family, my three sons, and I wouldn't move away from there for anything, but Chicago is the city of my youth. Munster, Indiana, is not far away, and my family would come to Chicago after Christmas to enjoy holiday sales. We made a few trips to Wrigley Field and Comiskey Park to watch baseball. Chicago takes me back in time, and, well, it's a hell of a fun town.

I walked up to Water Tower Place, basically the northernmost part of the shopping on Michigan Avenue, and checked out a few stores, stopped and bought some caramel popcorn, and was making my way back to the hotel. It was cold. The wind blew through my thick coat, and my face was becoming chapped. My feet hurt too. Walking on concrete was tough, even in comfortable, broken-in leather sneakers. I began wearing high-end leather sneakers a few years ago, and typically they hold up, but two or three miles of sidewalk strolling? I had debated putting on my running shoes for the night. I knew they ruined my outfit, but sometimes function needs to override form. I wished I had made the switch. I wanted to get back to my warm hotel room, take off these shoes, maybe go over my 10 a.m. presentation one more time, and warm up in the hotel shower.

A car pulled up next to me when I was a block from that warm shower. The window rolled down, and a gun stuck out at me.

"Hey, buddy, hop in." Stewart Givens smiled, like everything from a few months ago was some joke or misunderstanding.

"You fucking asshole," I started, not moving from my spot.

"Get in the car, and don't call me an asshole. I'm fucked, and I don't think shooting you will add any time to my sentence, so shut up and get in the fucking car." Yeah, two tough-talking, fuck-using orthodontists.

Stewart was driving a brown Crown Victoria, and the coupe door was heavy to pull open, rusted and old, it made a loud creaking plea for a squirt of WD-40 to its hinges. I felt the heat blasting when I moved to get into the car. Amazingly, instead of fear, I felt relief to be getting out of the cold.

Just after I sat down, but before I shut the door, I heard, "Do me a favor, Gabe. Leave your phone in the gutter before you get in." He waited for me to be comfortable before inconveniencing me, classic Stewart Givens. He wasn't pointing the gun when he asked, he held it in his hand on his lap.

I complied, walking back around the car and placing my phone next to a storm drain. I tried to conceal it, so a passerby would not pick it up and claim it. I heard Stewart chuckle behind me. "Can't afford a new phone, Gabe? Didn't buy the insurance?"

I didn't reply. I put a piece of trash over the phone and walked back around the large American made car. Once I was inside with my seatbelt buckled, Stewart pulled away from the curb.

We did not speak. He drove the speed limit, used his turn signals, and strictly obeyed all of the traffic laws.

I looked at the clock on the dash. It was 7:30 p.m.

"Sorry for the slow route we are about to take," he said, breaking the silence. "But I want to avoid cameras. I know highway 88 or 80 would be faster, but they have those pesky tolls." Interstates 88 and 80 are major U.S. highways heading west out of Chicago.

I did not respond.

He looked tired. His eyes were sunken, and he'd dropped ten or fifteen pounds. His head was shaved, and the hair that should have been on top was now a beard and mustache. He wore black-rimmed glasses, which I knew were fake. Stewart had perfect vision. It was the kind of stuff he bragged about, like anyone cared or could control their vision. All in all, he wore a pretty good disguise.

"I have some water, soda, and snacks. We aren't stopping to use a bathroom, so watch how much you drink." He used his elbow to nudge a white plastic grocery bag in between us. I didn't look, but I guessed it was filled with food.

"Are you going to share your popcorn? I can smell it." He was in a good mood, having nabbed his quarry. "Of course, you always were a selfish asshole, so I assume you will keep the popcorn for yourself. I'll have to take it from you, like I took your snooty bitch wife."

I'm sure he could see my jaw tighten. He might have heard my teeth grind, but I did not take his bait.

"I'm not sure how this night is going to end, Gabe, old buddy, but I do know I'm going to get some things off my chest, let you know the whys that have probably been eating at you for the last months." He grinned.

"I mean, it would kill me, wondering why my best friend did such bad things to me." He emphasized the words "bad things" in a funny voice.

He held his hands up and shook them back and forth for effect, like what he'd done wasn't actually so bad, that it was only my point of view. Like the whole situation—the rape, the kidnapping, the lying—was all about perspective, not true evil.

"Anyway, let's get out of Chicago, maybe even Illinois, and we'll get down to discussing the wrongs we've done to each other, hash out our differences, then I'll kill you, and we'll be done with it, but you'll know why it all happened. I'll give you that before the end." He smiled. "Oops, I guess I do know how this night is going to end."

I sat silently. The heat was cranked. I reached forward to turn the fan down. I did not remove my gloves, coat, or hat. I felt sweat gathering on my back, but I stayed wrapped up. I was worried Stewart would throw me out of the car, and I would have taken off my hat, gloves, and coat, and I'd be stuck in the cold, windy night without the proper clothing. I also hoped for a chance to run, and I would need my warm clothes then too.

You'd think I'd be scared, but I wasn't. Stewart Givens was a coward, and he was lazy. He had no follow-through. That's why he failed in his practice, and why he sucked as an employee. My biggest concern was how far out in the middle of nowhere he was going to leave me. He didn't have the balls to kill me.

I really wished I had put on those running shoes.

"Sure, make yourself comfortable." He encouraged me to adjust the climate settings. "I forgot you don't like a hot car. I just thought, you know, after walking up and down Michigan Avenue, you might be cold." Stewart reached forward and turned the temperature down to seventy. "That's better. I was hot too." He paused. "Yeah, I follow your practice on social media. Your office posted about your conference a month ago. I knew you'd want to walk up Michigan. I knew you'd be alone. You are so predictable."

I still did not reply. I was back to following the television or movie script, keep the bad guy talking, wait for my chance. What was the chance? What was I supposed to do? Yeah, no idea, but I knew I had to keep him talking, not that he was going to shut up. If there was one thing about Stewart, he never shut up.

"Except," he started, "you weren't predictable. You didn't act like you were supposed to act when I took Daniel. You fought for him. You didn't even like him. You hated that kid, my kid, and I know it. You didn't want him. You wanted Janelle, and you were forced to accept Daniel." His voice grew loud and he became upset. "My son was like the ugly friend some hot girl brought on your first date. You had to be nice to him, had to accept him, but you really could have thrown him out with the trash. You wanted your wife, that bitch who made you look like a fool, who spent your money, drank herself into oblivion, who was trying to kill herself." He had venom in his voice.

"Yet you fought for Daniel. I was happy to see it, but stunned and unprepared. Teddy and I had worked though all of the scenarios, all the situations that might arise from liberating my boy, and not one of them had you engaged and fighting to keep Daniel." He shook his head back and forth. "Man, you messed me up pretty well with that one, Gabe."

He stopped his rant for a while. I didn't know where we were exactly. It was a western suburb, and it was big. I finally noticed a sign indicating we were in West Aurora. The dash clock read 9 p.m. There were a lot of pauses in our conversation, if you could call Stewart rambling a conversation. I'll admit that I was in shock for most of this first hour and a half. I was dazed. Unprepared to hear him tell me I was going to be murdered. Despite the experiences earlier in the year, I was still an orthodontist from Cincinnati, and not a person ready to be kidnapped at gunpoint.

I also had a slowly growing suspicion he might actually kill me. Not full-blown belief, but a tiny iota of an inkling that Stewart might be crazy enough to follow through.

"Were you mad at me or Janelle?" I finally spoke. Stewart was right, I was curious as all hell to know why he did all of this.

"You," he replied.

That was it, one word, "you." He'd talked for an hour and a half about nothing, a bunch of random bullshit, and now he distilled his entire reasoning for rape, kidnapping, life on the run to one thing, a hatred of me.

I waited for him to say more. We sat in the car for fifteen minutes before he did. The miles west continued to click.

"You knew I was floundering. You knew I was screwed, and instead of taking me into your practice, instead of taking me on as a partner, you let me get gobbled up by that ortho-conglomerate. I was just some $100K a year employee. You think I could keep my house, cars, and country club on $100K a year? Could you?" I saw his knuckles grow white as he tightened his grip on the steering wheel.

"You never said anything." I defended myself. "I knew people were failing all over, but I didn't know you were in that boat."

He turned to look at me. "You had your practice manager call me and offer to buy my patients. The hell you didn't know."

Damn. I was busted, though I still tried to lie my way out of it.

"I didn't know that," I said meekly. "I'm sorry. That was an asshole thing to let happen. Dani was new. She was trying to make a go of our practice."

"Fuck you, Gabe. She was three years into the practice. Just own up to it, you greedy bastard. Admit that you cared about winning, about being the last ortho standing, and we can at least end our friendship with the truth. You had the best wife, the best family, the most lucrative practice. You had it all, top of the mountain, and you were only too happy to crawl over my dead body on the way up."

"You don't think our friendship ended before tonight?" I laughed. I actually laughed at the absurdity of his comment. I was in a car headed west. I was in the car against my will. A gun was pointed toward me. I'd been told I was dying later in the evening, yet I still laughed with incredulity at his comment.

"In the end I was just another orthodontist schlub for you to absorb. I was never an equal. We went to the same schools. We lived in the same town. We probably made the same money for a decade, but then you went big time, and you decided you were better than me."

Jesus, he was mad at me, and his hatred was palpable. How could we play golf together? How could we hug when we saw each other? It was obvious he wanted to beat me to death with his fists. I actually felt remorse for the way I treated him. His perspective was wrong, but if he had this much anger, well, as a friend I should have realized. He actually found a way to make me feel responsible for his insanity.

"Jesus," I mumbled. "You're right, I'm sorry. I screwed up." I sat in the seat, sweat soaking through my shirt, making it cling to my body under my heavy, black pea coat. My hands were dripping, and the inside of my lined deerskin gloves was soaking wet.

Stewart started to laugh. He was almost in hysterics at how funny the situation was. "Wow, maybe we should have talked five years ago." His comment made him laugh harder.

The road ahead of us was black. The glow of Aurora was a tiny spec in our rearview. The dark Midwest farmland stretched on both sides.

Stewart laughed for a few minutes. I noticed tears rolled down his face.

"Oh, shit." His laughing finally subsided. "Damn, that is funny. This is all one big misunderstanding. 'Sorry, Stew, my bad.' Priceless."

I was scared for the first time. That iota of thought I had before?

Stewart Givens was bat-shit crazy insane, and I was convinced he was going to kill me.

"You know, Gabe, it's amazing to me how you've rebounded. Again, Teddy and I worked through a number of scenarios, and in all of them, we ended up with Daniel, while you and Janelle were shattered and broken. It never crossed our minds that you would be so strong. Funny, huh? Plain Jane, Gabe, who lucked into Janelle, lucked into Dani to run his practice, lucked into his entire life, just bobs along with the tide, yet always seems to find port."

Stewart shook his head.

"Anyway, it was amazing to witness, your metamorphosis into a man. It was unexpected. Somehow you came out of the situation that was intended to ruin you, and became stronger, better, and happier. I mean, what the hell do I have to do?"

"This is all because I didn't take you in as a partner back in 2009? Are you kidding me?" The realization that Stewart was crazy, that he was literally insane, meant I needed to take the offensive. Sitting back, letting him rant, that was getting me nowhere.

Actually, it was getting me to Iowa.

"What do you mean am I kidding you?" he yelled. "Why would you ask me that?"

"Were you supposed to be an equal? Was I splitting my piece of the pie with you? Was Dani going to be 40% and you and I sat at 30% each? Do you expect Dani to take a cut because your worthless ass can't keep your practice running?"

"Worthless? So you are going to get me upset so I make a mistake?" Stewart laughed. "That's the plan? Keep me talking, wait for the mistake? Good old, predictable, movie-watching Gabe."

"I don't care what you think. I won. Winners take what they want. I took most of your customers anyway. You're the idiot who didn't accept my charity when Dani offered it." The truth was going to sting, but like he told me, I owed it to him before this was all over. "You obviously needed money, but your pride got in the way. I paid out close to $35K to one woman handing over her practice. That was five years' worth of country club dues. Who's the dumbass now?"

"I'm the dumbass? Who gave me the address of his drunk whore of a wife? Huh? Who literally handed me the keys to her crotch? I was floored when you asked me to help look for her. I mean, didn't you know I always wanted a piece of her ass? And then you introduce me to her pimp? Seriously? God, it was so fun fucking her."

"You mean the drunk, passed-out woman? Yeah, you are quite the man." I had nothing to lose.

"That's what people snickered about me, when, you know, they found out I couldn't have kids. I knew I could. I fathered a boy, a healthy, beautiful, strong boy."

So that was it. All these years, he and Teddy had tried to have children and couldn't. Stewart failed at his work and getting Teddy pregnant. I realized immediately that while Stewart was angry at me and Janelle, he was more upset at himself and the world.

"Have you been paying attention at all?" I stopped him.

"Paying attention to what?"

"We had Daniel tested. Rondo is the father, you idiot. You didn't father anyone." I took a chance he didn't know, that he was out of the loop while running for his freedom. "And as a side note, no one knew you couldn't have children. Most people who play golf all the time, and spend money on cars, they don't want kids. You're a selfish dick. I'm being totally honest, I assumed you and Teddy didn't want children. It never crossed my mind that you were impotent."

Stewart did not respond. I rattled him.

"And why is Teddy such a consolation prize? She's awesome. You got married before I did. It's not like you dated Janelle first and I stole her from you. What kind of revisionist history are you writing, Stew? Jesus, you stole her child. Didn't you see how we fought with the Rondos? How could you think we were just going to fall to pieces? Just walk away from a fight?"

"He's not my son?" Stewart's knuckles were a bright white on the steering wheel. "You dare to tell me he isn't my son? You don't think I know? You can say a lot of things to try and get out of your fate, but don't you ever say that again. I fathered him. I made that boy."

"Whatever, okay, fine, he's yours." I feigned compliance, making sure my voice let him know I didn't believe what I was saying.

I kept my eyes on his knuckles. I noticed some color slowly seep back into them. Stewart was calming down.

"Anyway, Gabe, my friend, my old school chum, I've had a lot of alone time for personal reflection. I've had some giant blocks of time lately to identify and work through some issues. You see, our friendship was always based on me being better than you, and I think it went off the rails when you passed me up." He turned to look at me. "I know, I know, that is a shitty thing to say, that you were my fat friend I kept around to make me look thin, but it's true. I got married first. I had a lower handicap." He stopped. "And I still do. I had a German car first, and our relationship was fine, but then you met Janelle."

He sighed a deep breath in and out.

"You met that beautiful, smart woman, and she was better than my wife, and suddenly I was jealous. Can you believe it? I was jealous of you. And you know why? Because she saw your potential. She molded you into what you are, made you complete." He wasn't making a lot of sense. I agree that Janelle made me the man I am today, but why would that upset Stewart?

My current strategy was not working, so I shifted gears. Instead of making him mad or regretful, I played into his ego. "Do you remember back in graduate school, I wanted to go into practice together? We had it all worked out, and then you balked. I was terrified, to be on my own. Here you were, opening an office first, having a beautiful, smart, funny wife first, buying a house, driving the expensive car, and I was struggling. I looked up to you. Why couldn't you be happy for me when it all worked out? Why aren't you happy for me now?"

"Because I'm not, I'm not happy for you, I'm jealous. I was supposed to have your life. You were supposed to be the ant, stuck working for some stupid company for peanuts, while I strolled around an office raking in money." Stewart grinned. "Do you know how happy I was when Janelle got fired? Oh, my god, it was like Christmas morning, and then she started drinking, and you told me she gambled all that money away?"

"What kind of friend are you?" I asked, stunned.

Stewart had turned the car onto different two lane roads several times since the lights of Aurora, followed by long stretches of straight away driving. His old car did not have a compass on the dash, and during the heated discussion I had lost my bearings entirely. It was dark all around us. Every once in a while I would notice a farmhouse with a front porch light turned on, but those were few and far between. We were in the middle of absolute nowhere. I wasn't sure if we were in Illinois, Iowa, Wisconsin, or Missouri.

"I was the friend who stuck to the big picture, the part of our relationship defined from the beginning, that I was better. You are the one who changed."

Stewart turned the headlights off, continuing to drive for a few minutes on back roads guided by the moonlight. I caught a glimpse of the clock just before the darkness, 12:30 a.m.

He rolled the car to a stop.

"I'm tired, Gabe. This life I've been handed, it sucks. I have no money. I have no friends. I have to figure out a way to get south, out of the country, maybe start over. I've been stuck in the U.S. until I could get to you, finish something I started. I wanted to destroy you, but you didn't cooperate, so now I'm going to kill you, weight you down, and chuck you in the river." His face was somber, as if what he was talking about was more obligation than enjoyment. "Your wife and family will never know what happened. You'll just disappear. Poof." He put his fingers to his lips and kissed them out.

"So get out of my car, and let's be done with it." He pointed the gun toward me.

"Why would I get out of the car? If you are going to kill me, I'm sorry, but you're going to have to do it in your car, get it bloody, leave some trace for the cops to discover."

He rapped the gun on my knee. It hurt, a hell of a lot.

"Ow, what the fuck, Stewart?" I winced in pain, rubbing my knee.

"I paid cash for this car. It's one of my only possessions. If I have to clock you over the head and drag you out, fine, but I'm not shooting you in the car." He pointed the gun at me again. "Get out of my car, just be a friend one last time."

He was insane. He thought we were still friends, like everything was as it should have been. I broke the rules. I exceeded my boundaries and outperformed him. This was my fault, all of it, and I could rectify some of it by doing him this one last solid.

"Fine." I opened the door, and I got out.

The cold wind hit me in the face, stinging as I tried to adjust to the elements after being in a warm car for five hours. The sweat running down my back chilled instantly, and I was shivering as I made my way to the front of the Crown Vic.

The ground under my feet was dirt, frozen farmland, stones bordered the side of the road. I heard a fast-moving river. We were parked on a road that ran adjacent to water, but did not cross. I wished there was a bridge, somewhere for me to run, but I was stuck. My knee throbbed, and I had a slight limp. Stewart could have run me down easily.

"Now that I'm at the end," he had to yell over the wind and river noise, "it's almost peaceful. I really am sorry. I'll get Daniel at some point, maybe a year, maybe two, when things have calmed down, but he'll be with his father."

I leaned over and picked up a large rock.

"What are you doing?" Stewart asked, shocked, amazed I wasn't on my knees in front of him, accepting my fate, perhaps begging for my life. "Put that down."

I walked toward him, despite the gun he held in his right hand. He waved it back and forth, gesturing for me to put the rock back into the field.

Or was his hand shaking?

"Hey, get away, stop," he pleaded. Stewart was not prepared, just like before, just like always. He didn't expect me to fight for my life, for Daniel, for Janelle. He was lazy, wanted the shortest path between two points. He didn't anticipate or want the work that comes with success.

He didn't take away the one lesson he should have from the summer. Don't threaten my family.

It's funny, because he had won. I was ready to die, to lie down and be done with it. I was tired, cold, scared, but then he talked about my family, stealing Daniel from Janelle, and I woke up.

I swung the rock and hit Stewart in the side of the head. I'm sure it made a noise, but I did not hear it. The wind blew too hard, and the river's roar was too loud. He slumped like a sack, went to the ground instantly. I expected the gun to go off, either because he pulled the trigger in self-defense before I struck him, or because his finger muscles tensed after the hit. The gun fell from his hand before he met the dirt. His finger had not been on the trigger.

It was a clear night, and I looked up at the stars. The light pollution from Chicago was long gone, and wherever I was the sky lit up like a million white Christmas lights. There was a good amount of moonlight, and I could see Stewart's eyes were open. I'd killed him, just like that, with a heavy rock to the side of the head.

I stood for a few moments, shivering, thinking, wondering why all this happened to me. I thought about dentistry school, and sitting in the food court that first week of classes, and the tall, attractive, popular-the-moment-he-stepped-into-the-first-lecture, man who sat down next to me and introduced himself.

"Stew Givens," he said, hand outstretched. My face was buried in a book, studying information I already knew, but wanted to know perfectly. I was excited to have a friend, and such a cool, popular friend.

I walked to the riverbank and threw the rock I held in my gloved hand. It had blood on it, already frozen in the cold autumn night.

I dragged Stewart's body to the river. I put rocks in his pant legs, used his shoelaces to seal the bottoms, and cinched his belt tightly around his waist. I put more rocks in his jacket sleeves, and zipped it tightly. I rolled my old best friend into what I later discovered was the Mississippi River, turning away as soon as his body was gone. I threw the gun into the river before walking back to the car.

It was low on gas, and I was nervous I might not make it to a station, but I did. I paid cash, kept my head down, but was not conspicuous. I figured out where I was, and I drove back to Chicago, making it to O'Hare by 5:30 a.m. I parked in long-term parking, went to the El train, and rode the Blue Line downtown.

I've never been arrested, never had my DNA collected or my fingerprints taken, and I'm hedging that wearing my gloves and hat kept hair, prints, and other evidence out of Stewart's car. I don't know, and I hope I never find out.

I made it to my hotel by 6:45 a.m., finding my phone neatly tucked under the trash I'd used to conceal the location. The phone was on, and I had two missed calls from Janelle. A text from her at 9:45 p.m. told me she was going to sleep and hoped I was having fun in the city. Dani sent me a "good luck on the presentation" text as well.

I assume the GPS showed I was at my hotel all night.

I typed in a message to Janelle, "sorry I missed you last night. Dead tired, went to bed, off to breakfast, love you, g."

I went to my room, showered, shaved, dressed for the conference, and made sure people saw me at the 7:30 a.m. breakfast. I drank a lot of coffee, ate some candy bars for sugar, and I nailed my presentation, getting a nice applause from the attendees and several questions afterward. I made a point not to limp or wince with pain, even though my knee was throbbing. At 3 p.m. I went back to my room and I slept until 5 p.m. I cleaned myself up again, and attended the ending reception, agreeing to share a cab to the airport with a new "friend." I flew home, and was sitting in my living room with Janelle at 11:30 p.m.

"We missed you." She sat on our couch in a flannel robe, her legs, clad in pink-plaid lounge pants, extending out onto a hassock, matching pink slip-ons covered her feet. I noticed a few Christmas decorations had trickled down from the attic; two nutcrackers adorned our fireplace mantel.

Daniel was in his bed, and the twins were finally asleep. They had stayed up late to see me when I came home. I rarely traveled, and it was a nice surprise and treat.

I looked at Janelle.

"Something happened," I said.

No secrets, no lies, we're in this together until the end.

"Daniel is safe, and so are you."

As incredible a writer as Edgar Allan Poe was, I do not hear the beating of Stewart Givens' heart. Most days it doesn't even enter my mind.

Made in the USA
Monee, IL
05 April 2022

94142092R00100